A Big Piece *of*
Driftwood

GERRY ELLEN

BALBOA.
PRESS
A DIVISION OF HAY HOUSE

Author Credits: Kate Bartolotta-editor, mentor, friend.
Thad Wages - supportive business partner.

Balboa Press books may be ordered through booksellers or by contacting:

Balboa Press
A Division of Hay House
1663 Liberty Drive
Bloomington, IN 47403
www.balboapress.com
1 (877) 407-4847

Because of the dynamic nature of the Internet, any web addresses or
links contained in this book may have changed since publication and
may no longer be valid. The views expressed in this work are solely those
of the author and do not necessarily reflect the views of the publisher,
and the publisher hereby disclaims any responsibility for them.

The author of this book does not dispense medical advice or prescribe the use
of any technique as a form of treatment for physical, emotional, or medical
problems without the advice of a physician, either directly or indirectly. The
intent of the author is only to offer information of a general nature to help you
in your quest for emotional and spiritual well-being. In the event you use any
of the information in this book for yourself, which is your constitutional right,
the author and the publisher assume no responsibility for your actions.

Any people depicted in stock imagery provided by Thinkstock are models,
and such images are being used for illustrative purposes only.
Certain stock imagery © Thinkstock.

Printed in the United States of America.

ISBN: 978-1-4525-9460-6 (sc)
ISBN: 978-1-4525-9461-3 (e)

Balboa Press rev. date: 04/16/2014

Acknowledgements

Kate Bartolotta – editor, mentor and innovative friend
Thad Wages – supportive partner and business aficionado

Gratitude and love for the following inspirational
souls: Becca Blay, Anna Harrison, Dee Dee Ritzinger,
elephant journal, Be You Media Group.

And to La Condesa-a woman who has guided me
my entire life, whether she knew it or not.

Contents

The Rest of Her Days

It was 2:30 a.m. and Rachel Harper couldn't sleep. All she thought about was what happened to her life. One minute she was wheeling and dealing in the real estate market in a prestigious city, and the next minute, she was sleeping in a sublet on the northwest side of a college town-with used furniture, no cable or internet, nothing that belongs to her, and lots of humility. This was her life, she thought. Ever since the real estate market crashed in 2008 in California, she had been scraping by to make ends meet. Her once charming lifestyle with her first husband and their luxury living had gone by the wayside. Now, she was submerged in singlehood, working odd jobs, dating a man who had a complicated life, and feeling a sense of wanderlust. It figures. She gets restless when life gets mundane. No amount of yoga or Pilates or meditation can squelch her desire to explore. Everything she had worked so hard for in the material world was now reduced to a lumpy borrowed mattress, a dirty couch with old cat hair from one end to the other, and a kitchen with only one pan to cook all her favorite dishes in. Lately, her legs were cramping from teaching too many boot camps to anyone and everyone who would pay her a nominal fee. "This is a pretty decent job," she thought. "It allows me to stay in shape, I can network with the pretty young people, and I can set my own hours". It was very similar to real estate in her mind, except she was barely surviving in her little month-to-month sublet. Although she was leasing a new small car, it paled in comparison to the 500SL Mercedes that she was accustomed to driving all through the neighborhoods meeting one client after another on a daily basis. When the real estate market took a dive, the Mercedes had to go, as did all her jewelry, electronics, fancy clothes, household items, and anything that wasn't attached to a structure. She was becoming environmentally conscious of everything, including her pocketbook. Ever since she left the island of Bali, on a long sabbatical to recover from everything she deemed disastrous, she wanted to recoup some of her dignity for what preceded it. The divorces, the uprooting from one city to the next, and even her real estate profession, where she had the honest intention of putting people in good houses and rolling in the dough in order to give back; it all lingered in her conscience on what to do next. She started to walk everywhere, mainly because she was concerned about gas prices and how often she had to afford a full tank just to get to one of her many jobs and back. Yes, this was the new Rachel Harper. She was a woman in her mid-fifties, with so much potential to climb back out of her rut and make something of herself. It was so important for her to be in the see-and-be-seen world again, that she attended every local community event, networked at coffee shops, sat in the bleachers at local kickball games (even though she didn't have any kids, or even knew of anyone who's kid was playing on the field at the time), and shopped at Whole Foods in the ritzy neighborhoods. Even that didn't make a difference in how padded her bank account looked. If anything, her bank account was constantly drained. Between the car lease, the sublet on the north side of town, and her desire to stay up on a similar lifestyle of days gone by, she was in the midst of a mid-life crisis at age fifty-three. And, this is the story of the rest of her days. As her life toppled from a very successful real estate broker to juggling the boot camp teachings, the night-time hostess job at a restaurant, and part-time assistant to a chiropractor, she was sure she could climb her way back on top. "Exactly what this looked like remains to be seen, yet somehow it will eventually complete a larger part of a journey I embarked on and lost sight of" she convincingly thought. She had bigger fish to fry. She was smack dab in the middle of her own personal crisis, as her therapist kept reminding her, and she was more than ready to hit the road when she felt the grass was always greener on the other side. She still had a wild streak. She still had time to burn. She still fantasized of the perfect outcome. She was still wondering how she managed to go from fairy tale romances, houses in the mountains, all kinds of money at her disposal, dogs who were her kids, and consistent travel; to a life of needing restoration and recharge on a faraway island, with nothing tangible to show for it. When she returned from Bali her loose plan was to somehow integrate the simple life into her old college city and start over. This time however, she was going to set the record straight as to where she lived, the job she landed, and a new uncomplicated mess of a relationship. She was on a larger journey, no doubt, as the rest of her days were dotted with one attempt after another to understand the depths of her failures. "I never actually felt as though living in Bali was tragic, I might add" as she filled out applications online. Her appearance was carefree and liberated. Nothing was ever too out of the question for a woman like her. She tried to align herself with people and places that resonated with how much fun she wanted to have. Growing up was not at the top of her list, as she had husbands to do most of the decision-making for her. With both of them out of the picture she was learning how to redefine herself through her words. She took up writing while in Bali, although she always had a pension for writing long love letters. She lived on the southern coast, the rainiest part, and worked odd jobs to make ends meet. She lived with several people in a large house, with what seemed like a commune, where they cooked together, did yoga, attended meditation gatherings, and rode bikes to the shore. She hung out on the crescent-shaped beach every day and was greeted by so many stray dogs. Since her dogs were no longer in her life, she welcomed the idea of having another dog when she returned to the mainland. The question was "when am I going to go back and what will that look like" were the words that started every journal entry.

After landing in her southern college city, a city that was on the brink of becoming a full-blown metropolis, she mentally prepared herself for the rest of her days. With only two bags in tow, skin as brown as a berry, crazy curly bedhead, and a body more fit than ever, she had to put one foot in front of the other.

The Job Interview

As she made her way through the city she called home, she was still wondering why she had chosen to work so many odd structured jobs. "This is not my passion at all", she mumbled to herself over a cup of hot green tea in the morning while pondering her next step. At least she felt she was keeping herself healthy and fit, amidst all the obstacles that she seemed to encounter every month. She knew she had a message to get out to the world; a purpose. She had a reason for living and being a part of this crazy Universe. She felt as though, sometimes, she didn't even understand herself, much less anyone else. Her passions were all over the place. She loved nature. She loved animals and the simplicity of their lives. She loved to run. She loved to do yoga at home (the only way to save money), and she loved to cook. But, there was one thing she was very good at doing, and that was to write. Her words were so eloquent, simple, and touched the lives of many. Ever since she was a little girl, she wrote the most exquisite letters to her brothers, and even boyfriends she wished were planning to stick around. Hell, she even wrote a Dear John letter to her husband, after he she admitted to having a one-night stand with a coworker. Despite the fallout of that marriage, she still felt compelled to write a letter and explain herself better. She felt as though the words on paper would make more sense to her husband and resolve the guilt that was still lingering deep inside her gut. Plus, she had the opportunity to return to the letter prior to sending it, and edit if need be. Writing and Rachel were a team. None of the odd part-time structured jobs could compare to her solo and creative time of writing. Although the jobs provided some interesting twists to stories and characters, it was her imagination that fueled her pieces of written work. She was becoming a master storyteller. "And, to live the life of a storyteller, one has to earn an income to afford the basics of life" her subconscious reminded her on a daily basis. So she set aside time each day, when she wasn't writing, to scour the ads on the internet, go to job interviews, and wait patiently for someone to give her a chance at making a decent living while nurturing her creative writing passion.

Looking for a job was a bit of an anomaly for Rachel. She had been at the top of the heap in real estate in previous years, and couldn't imagine herself stooping so low to work in a $10 hour customer service job. It was as if her entitlement aura and her scrimping persona were always in a battle. Although real estate was basically customer service, at least she was pulling in thousands of dollars each month to afford those luxuries that made her feel successful. "Ah, this is ego talking", she said, as she squinted to pluck her eyebrows in the mirror after a long hot shower. She used to have her eyebrows done by waxing and shaping professionals, yet now she was struggling to see every week to make sure she didn't leave a single brow behind, for fear she might have that uni-brow look. As her vision was now so compromised, and the small sublet didn't have a magnifying mirror, she had to put her glasses on just to make out one small hair on her face. "This is ridiculous" she thought, as she continued to pluck around the rim of the specs. She did have some vanity intact and she was grateful that she could even get up in the morning and look forward to putting herself together for the world to see. After that debilitating divorce and the successive nosedive of her pocketbook, she didn't want to lose any steam on how to get back on her feet. It has been years since her divorce and money woes, yet somehow the past three years haven't been that kind to her. "This year was going to be different", she thought. "I'm going to make something of myself, go with the flow, meet that life partner who supports my every endeavor, and possibly even buy a new Mercedes". She felt better just affirming these words to herself in the mirror every day, as she still couldn't shake the luxury lifestyle feeling. "Am I being selfish?" she asked the Universe after the detailed eyebrow session. It wasn't the little things that kept her going, but the feeling that a major change was getting ready to take place. She was now sensing an awareness she never quite felt before. Her soul searching for the past few years was showing signs that compelled her to continue with the spiritual practice of daily meditation. If anything, just sitting on the floor in full straddle split with eyes closed made her feel young and flexible. "Why shouldn't I be able to get the signs I need during this quiet time?" she thought out loud for all (including God) to hear. "Okay, my mission today is to find a job, go to the interview, wow them with my knowledge and presence, and walk away with exactly what I asked for". She didn't want to believe she had a strong ego, but she also felt she needed this confidence to even attempt to apply for jobs that drove her farther away from her passion for writing, yet ironically would provide more time for her writing. "This is such a crazy idea!" she kept telling herself, as she drove across town in the hopes of beating out the competition for yet another part time job. She needed some strong internal energy, as living in the college town for the past year has proven that the youth are definitely more on top of their game when it comes to job interviews and the application process. She was a bit jealous of this but since jealousy was one of the seven deadly sins she remembered from her early Catholic days, she decided to just be herself and do the best she could.

Deciding what to wear would be a start. She wasn't that much into corporate clothing, and didn't own pantyhose or heels, so whatever job she was planning to apply for had to make room for her very comfortable bohemian-style wardrobe. She couldn't see herself wearing makeup, fancy purses, matching earrings, coiffed hairdos, straight A-line dresses, or pantsuits, so she had a bit of a challenge on her hands, especially if she wanted to pull in a salary that would afford her life while she nurtured her freelance writing abilities. The first job interview was at a natural garden center. "This is the perfect place for me to commune with nature, wear jeans, get dirty, talk to interesting horticulturists, and learn more about indigenous plants" is what came to mind for her. As she drove into the vast dirt encompassed parking lot, completely unaware that her resume reads like a real estate and odd-job diary, she was hoping the manager would feel compassionate about her cause and her love of plants.

The woman behind the counter passed along a standard application to her and she sat in one of the tiny chairs next to the gardening book section to fill it out. "Hmmm, oftentimes, gardening centers hiring for part time help or even full time help, aren't interested in your resume" she mumbled to the nearest cactus. "They would rather have you fill out their application form, complete with everything that your resume basically states" she kept saying to herself almost loud enough for the staff to hear. It seemed tedious to her, but she truly wanted this job. The hourly pay was decent and she loved the idea of working at a gardening center. If anything, it would fuel more creativity for her writing. There was a questionnaire attached to the application, which asked for all kinds of knowledge regarding plants and their care. She used to have the most beautiful garden while living on the central coast in California, but those luxury days were long gone, and here she was in this college town not knowing what the indigenous flora happened to be gracing her presence. She had a thought. "If I call my good friend in California, who knows absolutely everything there is to know about gardens, surely she could help me on this test" was one scheme that she had during the garden application process. "The woman behind the counter is gone, I have my cell phone with me, and I can speak in a very low tone, while I call my friend and get the answers". Basically, she was going to cheat on her gardening application, in the hopes that no one would see or hear her. She made the call, it went to voicemail, and she thought her karma got the best of her. She was on her own to answer the detailed questions she had no clue about in the first place. It's just been too long since she picked up a shovel and deadheaded some flowers. "Damn" she thought. "A missed opportunity". In a desperate attempt to appear true to herself she flipped the application over to the back side, which was blank, and wrote a very heartfelt reason why she wasn't able to complete the questions that were asked of her on this test. She filled the page with word after word of her past gardening days, even mentioning some rare California flora (and fauna) in the hopes of impressing the manager and person in charge of hiring. The remainder of the application was easy, except she spent more time on the writing explanation as to why she didn't know the answer. It was all the native plant questions that stumped her brain and she did her best to explain her circumstances. She turned the application in to the woman behind the counter, quite proud of her multiple paragraphs of words regarding her current humility in the ill-forgotten gardening arena. She was sure she would get the job based on her honesty. At least she offered up three good references, her love of plants, her meager hourly requirement, and her punctuality on every job. "They have to see that I would be perfect in this place" was her silly subconscious talking while she drove away leaving a big trail of dust behind her. Despite the feeling that she somehow touched their hearts, she also knew that not knowing anything about current plant trends and care might not get her the job, so she continued her search.

She had another interview lined up with a culinary institute the following day. Because she was sending her resume to so many different types of work, she had the brilliant idea that working in a culinary institute would be awesome because she loves to cook, it would satisfy her insatiable desire to learn more simple dishes using the best and freshest ingredients, and just being around the kitchen environment would lend itself to domestic bliss. She had to don a more basic outfit for this interview due to the fact that the position required more managerial skills; something she had done in previous years at nursing homes and hospitals. The days in those depressing scenarios took a toll on her, but she met the most wonderful and diverse people she could ever have asked to work with during her late 20's. As she prepared for this interview, mapping where she needed to drive to so she wouldn't be late, gassing up the car, applying a little lipstick and mascara (two cosmetics she would not be without), she set forth on a new interview with a reputable culinary institute. When she arrived at the place, which was no more than a shopping mall strip, she wasn't entirely thrilled at the location. "I thought for sure that this would be more conducive to a campus or something" was her brain thinking softly over the loud rock and roll playing in her car. "Oh well, here goes my best foot forward" she sang to a blaring Led Zeppelin tune on the radio.

She was meeting with the two executives of the institute, and they didn't request she fill out an application or test. They had her resume in hand and simply interviewed her from that piece of professional linen paper. She fidgeted a bit in her chair, mainly because it was difficult for her to sit for long periods of time. Fortunately, she only sat during her writing times and meditation. At the culinary job she was to be on her feet all day, which she felt as if she liked and needed. Plus, she would be among so many fragrant and tempting herb and spice smells, which was the main reason for her applying in the first place. The two executives questioned her on her skills, her goals, her ability to lead a team, and her knowledge of technology. "Uh oh" she thought. "I have very limited technology skills, but I can pass those tasks along to other more well-suited individuals" was her mind going into overdrive. The woman executive seemed very congenial. She was the head chef and creator of the institute. The male executive flew down from their California office, and wanted to help in the interview process, in case she might need to travel to California to see their operation and how things are done. She overcame her anxiety and relaxed more into her chair. They asked her about real estate. "That doesn't apply to this position," her body language was saying. But the real estate and her ability to network and lead and be professional was what the executives were interested in. They felt she had a solid career and background and wanted to explore that. She answered every question with a very professional tone, confident in her demeanor, and a willingness that even surprised her. Deep down, she really wanted this job. Not only did her love of cooking come into play, but she felt a kinship with the woman head chef executive and the students who she met as she was leaving. The culinary institute job felt like she would have enough time to write, cook, and even conduct a relationship whereby her domestic skills could come in handy. The executives shook her hand as she left, and mentioned they would get back to her within two weeks with a decision. There were plenty more candidates to interview, but she felt she wowed them with her desire. "If only they could see just how much I want to work there" she shouted in her car as she navigated her way out of the congested shopping mall parking lot wondering if another rock n' roll song would strike her fancy.

A few days went by, and merely out of desperation, she couldn't stop checking her emails or text messages to see if any of these recent job foibles would actually take the plunge and hire her. As much as she felt confident in her abilities to work any job at this point in her life, she was still feeling unqualified for some basic tasks at work. Technology was her main weakness and stumbling block to any progressive job environment. Plus, she needed a pair of glasses to see almost every fine print item these days. Being in her mid-50's she was sure she could get by with store bought cheap specs, but now she needed some real prescription types that would be eclectic and cool. "If I have to start wearing glasses more often, they might as well make me look good and edgy" she surmised, as she perused the internet for more jobs. She did receive an interesting call back from a wellness center; as an assistant to the main chiropractor. This felt like a good transition back into her old profession, although she definitely retired from many years of teaching aerobics, boot camps, personal training, and just giving more of her energy than she was willing to do at this stage of her life. Being an assistant would make her feel more behind the scenes, a helper, in a non-managerial position, and continue with her true motivation to write a novel. She was ready for this interview. It was the last one in a series of daily interviews for the past week. And, she wasn't sure how much longer she could do this. "Job interviewing is a job in and of itself" she told her more responsible well-employed friends. They always rolled their eyes at her latest adventures, and some of them mentioned how they lived vicariously through her. She never saw her life as an adventure, per se; more like a documentary on what not to do when the shit hits the fan. So, she pounded the pavement in search of this wellness center position, put on mascara, lip gloss (not to be too fancy), and flatter shoes.

"After all, this isn't a glamour position, so I had better not over dress for the role" she told a friend with her phone to her ear, her head holding it on her shoulder while she kept primping in front of the mirror.

The wellness center was on the west side of town, in the hilly and nice green part. She was feeling good about it already. Surrounding herself with nature always felt more harmonious with her true self, so if she could work in that environment then surely it would be a pleasant experience. As she drove through the narrow alley to the tiny parking lot behind the stone and brick small building, which looked more like an old house, she felt rather excited and even more confident. "I can do this," she said, while exiting her small economical car and tossing her curly hair from side to side to give it that natural unkempt look. Walking into the front door of this wellness center house she was greeted by the receptionist, and at least ten other young applicants all vying for the same position. They were in all shapes, sizes, sexes, and ages. She sat up as straight as possible to give the chiropractor some insight about her perfect posture and positively supreme health. At least she felt this was the case. The receptionist passed Rachel a clipboard and a stack of papers stapled together. Even though she brought her resume the stack of papers had an application and two long tests to be completed within a certain time frame. "Ugh" she thought, as she flipped through the stack of papers and realized that the tests had nothing to do with wellness. After completing the application, which she felt was senseless based on the fact they already had her resume, she waited patiently for the receptionist to announce that the testing would begin. Meanwhile, the chiropractor entered the reception area and greeted everyone. He was a tall, handsome, athletic, and stately looking man. She felt she could work with this guy and possibly share her passion for writing and athletics and life. Somehow his demeanor seemed congenial to her and she was ready to take this test. As the receptionist announced "ready, begin" the applicants began their silence and perused one page after another of the most archaic and elementary math, science, geometry, and calculus questions. There were also questions pertaining to situations that had nothing to do with being a wellness assistant. "Is he joking with this stuff?" she mumbled to herself and loud enough for the other applicants to hear. It wasn't until one of the other applicants, the oldest woman besides herself who smelled of cigarettes, piped up and said "I feel like we are applying to be a member of the CIA!" She turned in her test, unfinished, and walked out. She buried her head in the exam and tried to reminisce on her high school days and just how much she hated tests and math and anything having to do with logic. This wellness assistant test was the toughest by far of any job interview she had been on the past week. Probably tougher than her real estate exam and she prepared for that. "Maybe my brain has turned to mush when it comes to these basic equations" she sighed in the midst of the younger applicants furiously trying to beat the clock. The receptionist yelled "times up" and everyone had to turn in their tests. She was about halfway finished; only this time she didn't write an essay on the back blank page as to why she couldn't finish the remainder of the test. She just let this one go. The tall and handsome chiropractor proceeded to take everyone on a tour of his operation, and from one tiny room to the next, each applicant hung on his every word, as if to feel as though they already got the job. She just slinked in the back of the pack and looked around at the décor. She never could quite pay enough attention to tours of any kind. That whole group thing lost her interest back in the many church days at Catholic elementary school. She was more interested in the paint colors he chose, the nice curtain panels, the lighting coming through the window, and the lavender smells emanating from the massage room. When the handsome chiropractor talked about potential hours the job would entail, she perked up, as this was important to her so she would be able to find the time to write and get creative. "Funny that I care more about my passion than actually earning a living" was the main thought occupying her mind at that moment. "Oh well, at least I gave it my best shot, wracked my brain for this testing stuff, and maybe the nice chiropractor will see that I had great posture while sitting" were the final silly thoughts in her never-ending brain missives. When the tour was over all of the applicants returned to their seats and finished up the front page of the pile of pages on their clipboards and she was the first one done. She wasn't sure if this was a good sign, but already she was putting way too much energy into this whole deal, so she turned in her pile of papers and clipboard, shook hands with Mr. Handsome, thanked the receptionist, and mentioned she had hoped to hear from them. A week went by and no response. Not even an email stating that they were still considering all the applicants and have yet to narrow it down to a few candidates. Why this infuriated Rachel is still baffling to her. She always felt as though a good employer should, at the very least, give the potential employee a heads up. This wasn't a good sign. She decided to let it go, take a slight job hunting break, and submerge into her writing. This was her thing, and she might as well work it on a daily basis if it was to be her main source of income down the road. So she committed to writing 1000 words per day, in any form or fashion. From journaling, to freelancing, to emails, to witty paragraphs about anything, to status updates on social networking sites, to novel ideas. Writing consumed her, and she gave it her all.

Now that she had attempted all the job interviews, and the searching continued on a daily basis, she was in a bit of a predicament. "How am I going to afford my basic necessities in life, like rent, car payment, and my one and only precious American Express?" These thoughts running through her brain on a moment-to-moment basis started to consume her world. A wise woman told her, not too long ago, to never worry about money or where it came from. She wasn't sure exactly how to do that, and still had those nagging thoughts every hour as to how to make money and afford her new vocation. Still, she needed to feel like a responsible working stiff and earn her keep. It certainly beat depending on others to foot her bills, which she had done many times in the past, yet in her newfound karmic cleansing lifestyle it was not going to fly anymore. She checked her social networking site to see if anyone had updated her or themselves on the latest happenings. There was a private message from an old friend she used to hang out with in the early San Diego days. This woman sent her a message about possibly staying with her while she needed to save some money for a few weeks. She had to process this information long and hard. "I remember when our dogs used to fight, the many laughs about men, and our similar interests. This could potentially work" was her gut talking at the time. Certainly saving money on rent would be optimum at this point, and until she landed a stable job to afford her own rent. The small studio by the lake that she was living in had an expiration date in a few weeks, and without constant money rolling in, she had to get creative. Her friend knew of Rachel's plight, sensed it, as she had posted a few hints on her social networking site; but was unable to actually come right out and say what was going on in her financial instability world. The timing of this private message from her friend was perfect. A few days went by and she responded. "Yes, I so appreciate you wanting to share space with me for a little while, and even though I don't have much to offer in the way of furniture, I can definitely bring lots of laughs, and help with your dog walking if you need it" she said with her tail between her legs. It was decided between the two old friends that Rachel would move in until she got back on her feet, which wouldn't be long she felt. "How grateful and lucky am I to have these wonderful friends to offer me some much needed help?" she felt in her heart. The remaining weeks went by on her lease, it expired, she loaded up her minimal belongings in her small economy car, and drove to the south side of town, in a nice neighborhood and moved in with her old Southern California friend, who happened to live in the same city as Rachel all this time and she never knew it. "Serendipity at its finest" she thought as she pulled in the perfect driveway that jutted out from the small perfect house. It was a scene right out of Pleasantville. The neighborhood had pristine green lawns edged to the inch of the sidewalk, pretty people walking their well-behaved dogs all over the streets, kids playing in the manicured parks, and plenty of open space and greenbelt areas to escape into nature and foster even more creativity for her writing. She felt very blessed and grateful. This phase of her life was just beginning. Despite the humiliation of not being able to afford rent anymore, she was even more determined to find that well-paying job, help her friend with groceries, cooking, cleaning, and dog walking, and move out within a month or less. She also knew that her boredom on any structured job was actually the gateway to serendipitous experiences and the most creative mind possible, so she factored that in with her decision of where she would work, even part time. When she finally landed a position in a retail vitamin store, she felt as though she could contribute to society in a normal kind of way. The Universe had an entirely different plan.

Staying with a Friend

When she decided to move back to her college city and go on the many job interviews, she needed a place that doubled as a launching pad. Having her old friend, Carla, offer her home as somewhat of a refuge for as long as she needed was a blessing in disguise. "Hey Carla, thank you so much for your kindness in allowing me to stay with you" she silently whispered into her cell phone while driving the rental car over to the south side of town where Carla was living. She never enjoyed chatting on the phone while driving. It made her feel less focused on the radio piping in fun music, and the road itself. "No problem at all" said Carla in a seemingly curt fashion. Sensing Carla's vibe, she was already thinking she might have to stay at a motel for a few days until she got back on her feet, but the reunion with Carla and her home proved otherwise. "I'll only be there until I get a job and my own place to live" she mentioned to Carla while fidgeting for lip gloss from her small clutch while still driving south. She was now a roommate. Both women in their early 50's and cohabitating together seemed almost daunting, as it did exciting. Rachel's friend, Carla, was a full-time working woman. She spent ten hours per day in the healthcare field, toiling away amongst the sick and needy at a local hospital. "That must take a toll on her life and psyche and energy" she felt, as she harnessed up the dogs on their leashes for their first walk with her in charge. Carla never asked her to participate in helping at all; she just felt obligated to provide any help she could, as Carla was so kind in giving her a place to rest her head for a few weeks. "And, a comfortable place it is" she mused to her mother over the phone on one of their many monthly check-ins. As Carla exited the house at the crack of dawn every morning to tend to her patients, Rachel was finding ways to repay her by being domestic. Each morning she would open up the blinds to the fairly dark house, which surprised her given that Carla was pretty outdoorsy, but what this perfect house lacked in sunlight during the best parts of the day, it made up for in room and space and some fine accoutrements. With all the gratitude and comfort she could summon, she leashed up the dogs and ventured out the door to explore the neighborhood and the nearby greenbelt. "These dogs are rather unruly on the leash; wonder if I could just unhook them and let them be free" was always on her mind when it came to leashes, dogs and freedom in general. Walking the dogs, cleaning the dishes, perhaps vacuuming up some dog hair that accumulated in all corners of the rooms, having the doors open to allow sunlight and happiness into her environment, and looking for jobs; this was her rose-colored glasses life for the time being and she was enjoying every moment of it. Even attempting to roll out her yoga mat and get quiet and contemplative was fulfilling, except the dogs always managed to slobber on her during a downward dog or corpse pose phase. She didn't mind. She was just feeling so lucky to have a place to call home, if even for the time being.

Every late afternoon when Carla returned home from work, she always wanted to look busy, or have potential job news to report, or talk about what the dogs did for the day, or have dinner ready, or just not even be home. She never wanted to appear as though she was taking advantage of the welcomed situation and Carla never gave her that feeling; it was her own conscience that was playing some tricks on her. "One might call it guilt," she admittedly said to the dogs one day, but she never wanted to admit that guilt was creeping back into her psyche, especially with all the inner work she had done since her divorce. Guilt and shame were the biggest obstacles for her growing up. That whole Catholic syndrome plaguing her since she was a small child took eons to overcome, and here she was again, feeling somewhat guilty of not punching a clock as of late. "Oh well, I'm doing the best I can" she surmised on an hourly basis while basking in the sun sitting on the backyard patio chair among the flowers. Carla had a great house and had owned it for seven years. She had to admit that she was a bit envious that her good friend had accomplished such success, yet her idea of success was being redefined every single day. Since she was devoting her time and energy to her vocation of writing, even having stainless steel appliances no longer mattered to her. Just having a comfortable bed, running clean water, simple healthy food, pretty natural surroundings, and a solid intention were at the forefront of her heart these days. She even felt good about attesting to not having much. It used to be that owning a home, having the luxury auto, and being able to afford the nice restaurants defined her in the early real estate booming days in California. Now, when she runs into some old colleagues or rich friends, she no longer hangs her head in shame. If anything, she is grateful, enriched, and very satisfied. She has sort of grown up.

A few weeks went by, the two older roommate women had so much fun catching up on the news most evenings, watching smut shows, dancing in the living room to old school rock and roll, making easy going meals that consisted of cherry tomatoes, olives, and cheese chunks, walking the out-of-control dogs in the evening under the stars and moon, and talking about past lovers. Carla's dogs were so strong on the leash that every moment a squirrel or cat would cross their paths, she would end up in the bushes with them on the other end of the leash. Carla even broke a leg one time trying to hold the dogs off from a rampant cat chase. "Now I can totally see what you mean about these two dogs" she said to Carla on an evening walk. "I got your back should they go after a critter" she followed up with, and the two of them laughed so hard their bellies ached. When they spoke of men it was always a rant of a topic. Rachel was involved in sort of a complicated mess of a part-time relationship and Carla was dissing men altogether after her ex threatened her with a gun, so both women had plenty to laugh about. Plus, being in their menopausal years they swore that past mistakes were never to be repeated, what with all the wisdom they had now.

Because it had been years since she owned a television, she enjoyed snuggling up on the couch most every night watching some random show with the dogs, her friend, Carla, and a cup of tea. She felt as though Carla was a bit lonely, and all her ranting at the T.V. during the political news shows made her a bit crazy in the beginning, but she just laughed to herself and appreciated the differences between the two women. She had never seen Carla so passionate about politics or woman's issues, so it was a new twist to their friendship. But, as time went on and no job was coming into fruition for her, she started to feel the pressure of needing to move on and away from Carla's energy. Despite all the weeks of fun and laughter, she knew this comfortable lifestyle wasn't forever. Carla never wanted a long-term roommate and Rachel didn't want to be a burden. "Have you started looking for places to live?" Carla casually mentioned most every day when she came home from work. "I have a friend coming into town who needs a place to stay" she continued in a passive-aggressive way. One Sunday afternoon when she returned home from a long run on the nearby trails in the Pleasantville neighborhood, Carla wanted to have the talk. "I think you need to tell me what your plan is" said Carla very directly as Rachel was sitting on the barstool counter sipping on a coconut water. "I totally understand where you are coming from and I plan to move out by the first weekend of February" was her rather abrupt response. The tension was palpable. It had now been two full months of living together and the beginning of February wasn't approaching for another week, yet Carla was getting antsy. Somehow she was feeling the pressure of having another person in the house not living the same working lifestyle, who didn't share her political rants, and felt the dogs were always tired and overworked. Their differences were beginning to shine. It was inevitable, as she thought back to how their friendship ended in previous years; on for about three months, then off for about fifteen years. It didn't bother her at all; what bothered her most was the fact that she didn't really have a plan B as to where to go. Her complicated boyfriend was no help and she wondered what the hell she was doing in this relationship with him in the first place. After all, he was to be her salvation after her return from the much-needed sabbatical on the island. "Wrong" she pouted to herself. This relationship of hers was still marred with one false promise after another. The only good that was happening within their togetherness was the fact he had a truck and helped her move most of her boxed up items to and from storage. God knows she made more than fifty trips to that storage unit, and with the help of her complicated boyfriend, she at least felt like she wasn't alone in all the unsettledness of late. She packed up the last of her clothes, toiletries, vitamins from the refrigerator, and assorted teas from the kitchen cabinet. She set aside all these boxes by the garage, so Carla would get the sense that she was in fact on her way out the door for good. Something shifted in Carla and Rachel wasn't sure what, but there was always a vodka bottle stuffed behind the blue corn chips in the pantry that had Rachel wondering what was going on. On some nights when they walked the dogs, Carla would stumble around, slur her words, and her breath did smell of alcohol. Since she had a keen sense of this, given her past husbands' battle with alcohol and previous relationships that never tried to hide their addictions, she knew that Carla perhaps had a bit of a problem that she was not addressing. It never came up in conversation, but the way Carla approached her regarding the move-out date did seem to come out of left field. "Thank you so much for everything, Carla; I will keep in touch down the road, and I owe you a birthday dinner in the upcoming weeks" she said as her and the complicated boyfriend drove off in his truck with her packed life in tow. She never heard from Carla again, and it was just as well. Political season was ramping up and she wasn't keen on getting involved with the know-it-alls in that arena, so not being around Carla during that time was a blessing in disguise. Her life was moving on. How she got to where she was going was another adventure altogether.

The Fiat

When she decided to make the college town her life post-divorce and relinquishing all of her possessions through garage sales and pawn shops, she was in desperate need of some transportation. Not having a car after returning from her island sabbatical proved to be a bit more stress than she had bargained for in her new/old habitat. To be able to move around the city, get from one place to another to see friends and buy groceries or sit at a coffee shop and use the internet; not to mention needing wheels once she landed that job that would alleviate all of her debt at this point, she was now contemplating the next move with a shiny car in the picture. "Should I rely on the bus since it's a cheap way to go and I would meet lots of new people?" she thought as she perused Craigslist for inexpensive means of transportation. "I really don't want to take on a car payment, car insurance, and all that goes into owning a car" she rebelliously surmised. "Maybe I'll just rent a car for a few days, figure it out, go on my job interviews, and decide whether the bus would drop me off near my job." "Or, I could purchase a bicycle and commute that way, lose a few pounds, suck in car exhaust, see the city like a dog with my head out the window, and arrive to my destinations feeling alive and energized!" was the newfound attitude she had adopted at that moment. It didn't last very long, as she thought of the unavailability of bike lanes in the city and how odd that was given the nature of the supposedly healthy city, and the fact it was really just an old college town. She decided to rent an economy car for ten days and go from there. All the while, she was booted out of Carla's house, amicably of course; and sent to a dinky hotel on the north side of the city until she could figure out where she was planning to sublet. There was so much happening simultaneously, needing transportation, needing a place to live, needing a job- you would think she was overwhelmed. She was quite the opposite, as all of the spiritual work she had embarked upon for many years after her divorce enabled her to reach a certain level of contentment, and this kind of stuff just rolled off her back. She was bummed out about her new situation; but she didn't let it get to her. Instead, she found herself at the nearest Enterprise car rental place, which happened to be walking distance from her dinky motel. She rented an economy car for 10 days. The economy car had not been exactly what she signed up for, but she was ready for anything that was cheap and wouldn't obliterate her first months' rent funds. As it turns out, a brand new Fiat sporty car showed up for her on the rental lot. It was red, flashy, small, and a stick shift. "What fun this is going to be!" was an exuberant Rachel smiling to the car rental man. He warned her that it doesn't have much pick up and go, but it gets great gas mileage, is safe on the highway, and she'll end up wanting to buy one when the 10 days are over. "Yeah right, like I really need a car payment at this point" she said to herself while the car rental man was swiping her credit card for approval. She had a full tank of gas, only 200 miles on the odometer, a pretty decent radio, a somewhat spacious back seat for whatever she needed to transport, and a fun attitude to go with the color of the car. She completely forgot this was only temporary and her future plans once the 10 days were over. "I'll cross that bridge when I come to it. By that time, I'll have a good job, a place to live, and will be able to afford to buy a car outright, if need be" she whispered to the empty passenger seat as she fiddled with the radio stations. The little Fiat was the wave of the future. She didn't see many on the road and that was just fine with her. Being unique and different was always optimum for her anyway. She just had no idea it would translate into a rental car as well.

She felt so nifty driving around town in the bright red Fiat. She purposely drove to places she would never frequent, just to be seen. She would bop her head up and down in the drivers' seat while listening to the radio turned up at full blast; to show the other drivers on the road that she was young, hip and happening. For some reason, the little Fiat car that looked like a small bug gave her a sense of liberation and youth. In the college town (which began to grow by every second into an overcrowded city) it was precisely what she needed to feel part of the scene. "If I'm part of the haps here in this place, I might as well drive a haps car" she said with some sort of urban dictionary feel to her words. It reminded her of a recent writing gig she just accepted as a freelancer online where she was commissioned to write some small blurbs for a mobile app that would appeal to the twenty-something's who drank a lot of beer, ate pizza, and partied all night. It was a diversion from her recent freelance writing gigs, but she welcomed doing something out of her comfort zone, and writing a few mobile apps might be just the diamond in the rough she needed to take her in a well-rounded writing direction. The more variety she had in her vocation the more she felt she wanted to write. Focusing on the same topic week after week was becoming a bit boring for her and she was happy to delve into a different arena. She was now driving a youthful car and she felt that writing for youthful mobile apps would suffice. It was all part of some sort of plan that she had, yet she never knew how it was all going to turn out, which was just fine and dandy with her. "Expect the unexpected" she always said to herself and her friends.

The 10 days came to an end for her bright red Fiat rental vehicle. She fell in love with the car. She had never been attached to a car, per se, but the small rolling red machine on the road captivated her, and it was so much fun. She found herself turning in the rented vehicle, catching a lift to the Fiat dealer in town, and leasing one herself, with barely any money or auto insurance. She had never leased a car before, as most of her previous automobiles were either hand-me-downs, purchases by her husband, or a used car. It was all so very empowering to her. She had negotiated a three-year lease, did all the paperwork transactions herself, patted herself on the back for having stellar credit and the wherewithal to save just enough money to put down the first payment and get some recommended car insurance. As much as she swore off the car ownership idea, driving around town in a Fiat made her feel adventurous. And it was an economy car, so that also felt good, as far as the environment was concerned. She opted for the "verde olivo" color, which was a metallic olive green vehicle she plucked right off the showroom floor. It reminded her of when she traveled to Italy eons ago and how many free olives she ate after a siesta; "so why not just go with this color green?" she told the salesperson on the floor, while also mentioning her Italy trip. The salesperson acted interested in her stories, but just wanted to reap the benefits of the sales commission, therefore she speeded up the process before she could change her mind. She could care less that Rachel traveled to Europe by herself for the first time. Having leased her Fiat right then and there made her feel powerful and in charge. The only addition she wanted was a sunroof. For some reason that extra purchase made her feel as though this was a step away from those old luxury autos she used to have with all the bells and whistles. She questioned why she needed to go back in the past to that memory, as it seemed beyond her; but she was an evolved woman at this stage. Probably more so in her mind than in her actual pocketbook, and some other actions she's taken where others still scratch their heads. After about two full hours with the entire car leasing transaction, she had a massive headache. Between number crunching, calling the car insurance company to obtain coverage on the spot, talking to everyone who congratulated her on the new purchase, a few posing photos by the dealership promotions board, and basically her own mind wondering what the hell she had gotten herself into, she forgot that a lease is basically renting a car. She didn't own it. She didn't truly buy it. She was renting it for three years, and if she decides to move again for an extended period of time, or she just doesn't have the money to maintain the vehicle, a lease is much more difficult to exit. "Why didn't I think of all these things, silly impulsive me?" she thought as she fumbled with her belongings in her purse in search of some much-needed lip gloss for her dry mouth and peppermint oil for her headache. "Oh well, at least I can have someone takeover the lease in case I decide to move to the islands again" was always her copout self-talk. She was going to keep the Fiat for as long as she could. It suited her lifestyle and was just damn cute.

Day after day, drive after drive, riding in the Fiat took on a whole new meaning. She never felt as though a car defined her, but she truly loved the new Fiat. She pictured a big furry non-shedding dog in the back seat, an interesting literary agent in the front seat who she could shuttle around with that dog, a few necessary items in the spacious hatch trunk area, the sunroof always open so she had that California dreamy look going, and practically a new lease on life. She felt it was strange how a little metallic, rolling, sporty, Italian olive made her feel so special. "It was the only thing I have going in my small material world, so why not relish in the luxury?" she rationalized on a daily basis. The odd thing is she only drove the Fiat to work, the grocery store, and maybe a friends' house for dinner. Otherwise, she walked everywhere. After months of walking and catching a bus and sitting on curbs waiting while her feet needed a break, she thought she might just as well keep up the walking habit, as it suited her fine. She saved so much money on gas, as the prices at that time were seemingly skyrocketing and almost $4 per gallon. The Fiat wasn't sucking up too much petrol, it's just that her wallet wasn't as padded as she would have liked and spending on gas seemed odd to her. In order to keep the Fiat she had to afford all those oddities, like car insurance, oil changes, gas, smog inspections and the like. "Silly car" she chuckled every time she drove off to meet a friend for dinner or lunch. She was kind of a social butterfly, as independent as she was; yet she definitely loved her solo time at home or out and about. Most people liked to hear what she was up to via social networking; simply because she had some crazy schemes always in the works, and she was in the throes of publishing some pretty decent articles for magazines. Her close friends also wanted to hear the latest greatest job that she landed, while nurturing her writing vocation. She always had a story to tell her friends regarding a job, whether she stayed employed or not. Most of her friends were all either in the corporate world, or were creative artists in some form or fashion. She had a very wide spectrum of people in her inner circle and they all meant something important to her. She relied on her friends for every ounce of loyalty, responsibility, honesty, and goodness. Fortunately, she was never short of any of these qualities herself, so she tended to attract like-minded souls who were always rooting for her. "How lucky am I to have such cool people in my life over the years?" she said to herself in the mirror on a daily basis. She was one lucky gal and after a somewhat bitter divorce, and many of her so-called friends splitting to side with her ex-husband, she now had an incredibly enriching future to look forward to. Her close clairvoyant said that to her many years ago and she still hears those words in her head swirling around, as if all the signs and symbols meant something in her current life. She was quite the dreamer, always having many fantasies and dreams. "I need a little reality check every now and again" she told her nearest and dearest. Each time they offered words of perspective or alternative opinions, it set her straight and she was good to go. Fortunately, she now had a Fiat to take her there.

Self-Care Heaven

*M*any days and months had passed and she had found a rather cool furnished sublet that didn't break her bank. She had settled in nicely, living among the shadiest and hilliest neighborhood with lots of healthy trees, and upbeat neighbors who were half her age. They weren't always quiet, but she appreciated their enthusiasm for every single day of living, piping music in from all corners of their condos, greeting each other with fist bumps, and constantly feeding the nearby feral cats. She had a big oak tree to shade her apartment to keep her utility costs down in the brutally hot summers, all the basic amenities that she needed at this stage of her life, a big bathtub, a somewhat comfortable bed (because God knows her previous sleeping arrangements left her with something to be desired and a constantly sore back), and sweet little dogs that live in the complex with the ability to chase all the feral cats. She was doing okay. She could and would walk to the nearest coffee shops and use their internet, walk around to explore and be in nature during dusk, and walk to the drugstore and movie rental box, which were both side by side. She walked everywhere. Despite the new rolling olive Fiat parked under the large shaded oak tree just waiting for her to start it up, she preferred to be on foot. The rolling olive had to sit there many days accumulating tons of bird crap on the windows and paint job. She would wash the Fiat often, park it back under the oak tree, and continue to walk everywhere. She would only drive the car to work and back. "Seems almost silly to have a car, but I need it for the clock-punching job" she told her mom on another one of their monthly chats. Her new job was at a local integrative pharmacy, so she was constantly on her feet all day, helping people while standing on concrete floors for eight-plus hours. Even though she was in reasonably good shape, her feet began to thoroughly ache at night. Every first step out of bed in the morning, her feet had some excruciating pains. "I wonder if I have plantar fasciitis again" she thought every morning while rising out and getting ready to meditate and do some yoga before driving the Fiat to her new job. She also enjoyed running a few days per week, to keep her older body in good health, her mind clear for the days' activities, and it just helped her process thoughts of the day, either what was coming, or what had passed. Her feet now hurt quite a bit. "And all this time I felt being on my feet would be a good thing, meeting and greeting people all day, and taking a break from writing most of the hours" she rambled onto the empty air of her new apartment. Needless to say, she gave up her treasured biweekly pedicures after her real estate job tanked, due to not only the cost, but the women who worked on her feet never quite paid attention to her request to "go easy on the toes, as I run quite a bit, I'm on my feet all day, and I have sensitive nerve endings". It didn't help. Every pedicure was a constant diatribe to someone new on what she was able to tolerate. The women listened, but did what they were trained to do and pretty much gave her enough unease to where she would grab the handles of the massage chair every single time to alleviate the pain. She flinched so much that any amount of relaxation and therapeutic benefits went out the window. That, and she would always mess up the pedicure when she sank herself into the Fiat so the big toes always needed to be redone. The women in the pedicure salon would roll their eyes, speak in their native tongues, and she knew they were slamming her for being such a difficult client. "I paid good money to have my toes prettied up here, the least you could do is just touch up the big ones, please?" was her plea as she slumped back into the chair, somewhat humiliated, and feeling like her ego got the best of her. The women continued to talk and laugh and she just knew they were making fun of "that crazy American". She didn't leave until her toes were done perfectly and she even waited an extra amount of time for them to dry before once again, trying to slink into the Fiat without screwing up the big toes. More often than not, she had success; it was just those days where the redo far outweighed any rewards for a job well done.

The rain continued to saturate the earth in the seemingly hot climate, yet she was thrilled with the change in weather. She was not a huge fan of months of humid heat with temperatures soaring beyond 100 degrees every day, so donning a rain coat, a long sleeve, and long pants suited her just fine. The only mainstay in her simple wardrobe was her flip flops. She wore them daily. With the exception of the rule of close-toed shoes for work, she would wear flip flops every single day of her life. And in recent years, she has done just that. Now that she was in her 50's high heels hurt her back, close-toed shoes make her feel claustrophobic and hot, and she could care less about being a fashion plate. As often as she loved to get her toes and feet worked on, the only necessity in her current line of shoes and clothing was a quality flip flop. Not just any old sandal made of rubber and nylon, but the kind that had support, good tread on the sole, came in multiple colors, and felt like pillows on her feet. She had been known to even wear flip flops to elegant weddings. She just made sure they had some sort of adornment or patent leather strap, or were decorated with intricate accessories beyond a small label. That was all she cared about, and "screw others who don't like what I put on my feet!" was her subtle rebellious mantra she said every time she slid her overworked feet into one of those comfy things.

Self-care was a big deal to her. Massage, spa treatments, long hot baths, aromatic scented anything, tantric anything, and treatments that could even go beyond the unusual and rare, appealed to her at this stage of her life. Most of her limited paychecks were applied towards these measures, and she never apologized to the Universe for spending that kind of money. It mattered to her and she felt her health was priority. Sanity and serenity were top notch for her too, but the thought of a stranger deeply rubbing her back and tender points was always the type of energy work she needed to continue a creative life. Her husband used to buy her gift certificates for most of the basic treatments, such as "queen for a day" type of things, but there was always this sense that she had to return the favor in some way. She never had the money to spend like he did, but she wanted to assure him that she was on board with the whole giving and receiving aspect of life. The problem for her was she couldn't afford to give in that way. She would have preferred to massage her husband with oils and potions herself, yet every time she would attempt this relaxing love-fest, her husband fell asleep and she wasn't sure he was soaking in all the pleasures, so she would quit the massage; or, she would get bored with him not cooing with "oohs and ahhs" at her magical hands. She had no training at all; it was more of a feel for what he needed and she just went from there. After a few sessions of her home-style massage treatments, her husband ended up going back to his professional woman who would pretty much tear up his muscles and give him that satisfaction that he sorely craved. There was no sexual tension in his paid massages, but he always returned home with greasy hair around his neck, a few sheet creases in his face, and a desire to do nothing. She never massaged her husband again, and she put that in the negative column as to why they weren't suited for each other in the long run. She loved to give back and that was one way of showing her gratitude. If it wasn't appreciated she would get upset. But her expectations were something she needed to explore altogether. Over the years she had learned that depending on someone else to please her and make her happy was a recipe for disaster. She was a self-made woman, and being in her 50s was her time for renunciation. She started to perform her own manicures at home, after a few failed attempts at having to sit for extended periods of time at the nail station when getting the professional manicure. She opted for the French version, as it made her fingernails look natural and beautiful, and still somewhat ritzy. But for her, the price to pay was she would inevitably mess up her expensive manicure as she exited the salon. She even resorted to waiving her free hand out the sunroof of the Fiat to make sure that the hand drying process was secure. That got old for Rachel. When she discovered that she had the patience to do her own fingernails, she walked over to her nearest drugstore (she loved knowing she could walk to everything she needed without having to spend gas money for the Fiat), and bought all the necessities for a quality manicure. As simple as this seemed to her, the best part was her hands looked healthier and more authentic than ever and she saved a sizeable chunk of her paycheck from the structured vitamin job to pay for other little pleasures. Her toes were a different matter altogether. She was not going to give up pedicures as long as she had to display her feet every day in flip-flops. Pedicures made her feel empowered in some strange way. She had no plans to cease this habit, as simple as it was to her. She proclaimed to friends she might even attempt a home version someday, but the message was always clear. "Take care of myself, and the Universe will take care of me" were her thoughts as she exited yet another nail salon in search of the perfect foot treatment.

With the onset of autumn and the leaves beginning to fall, and the always oppressive heat and humidity of summer days ending, she was more than ready to usher in a new season. There was this feeling of new beginnings in the air, a transformation taking place on a subterranean level that she felt very deeply. It is not just within her being but the world at large. What motivated and inspired her on a daily basis during this time of year is the exuberance and carefree nature of a child. She noticed all the elementary kids running around during the school hours, spending time in nature on the playground, razzing each other and letting off some steam. She passed the young children every single day on her morning walks and runs, and smiled from ear to ear as the kids taunted each other, ran in circles on a makeshift dirt track, hung on the jungle gyms like human monkeys, yelled and screamed as they chased one another around the grassy playground and amongst the trees. It reminded her of how rebellious she was at that age; how she was the stand-out tomboy girl for being kind of a maverick in all playful situations. Her imagination and creativity, even at that age, began to shine and rumble within her belly. She always remembered her days as a kid, and venturing near the school playground reaffirmed her memories. She always felt inspired by the freedom of a child. It was similar to her adult days when that black-sheep side of her would rear its ugly head and she would give in to playing the part of a bratty kid. It wasn't her best days; more like her dark days, but she learned a great many lessons by allowing herself to be in that moment, although she never knew it at that time. It also brought her to the feeling of the freedom of an animal. She was passionate about animals and nature. When she lived in her large spread on many acres in the mountains she had all the freedom in the world for her animals. She had four dogs who could roam free without the confines of city life. She never owned a leash and felt somewhat entitled when people passing by would yell at her to leash her dogs. She was more like the pied piper, always corralling the dogs in her presence, and being quite relaxed and successful at it. This mattered to her because her dogs were very well-behaved on the mountain, except for the occasional chase of deer, coyotes, or other wild critters. The faraway neighbors would comment when they saw one of her dogs on a nearby trail, treeing a raccoon or some other small varmint. She never let it get to her, nor did the neighbor. It was merely a casual exchange of mountain people pleasantries. She did have a row with a few conservative mountain types who barricaded their property from any trespassers and were round-the-clock watching for those who would break the rules. "I think we'll be okay today" she said to the dogs as they scampered by the guarded property on crisp mountain mornings, hoping none of them would get shot, as the neighborhood was a bit gun happy.

Smelling the cooler air, the breezes on a crisp morning, and the clouds taking on shapes and colors that only a new season can discover gave her a tremendous amount of hope and excitement. She thought back to when she was about ten years old, living at the end of a cul-de-sac on a busy street in a big city and riding around on her new Schwinn bike with a sparkly blue banana seat. Her bike had a pretty white basket with flowers adorning the front and always a doll sitting in that basket with perfectly matched clothes and newly cut hair. She had a thing for cutting her dolls' hair, as she once imagined herself being a hairdresser in her adult life. Her mother questioned her all the time about why she needed to borrow her sewing scissors, and never understood how she would take a brand new doll with luscious long fake hair and chop it off to some strange bob cut. She never had an explanation for her behavior at that time; she just loved to do it. "Yes, I was deemed crazy by many" she mused to some stranger at a street corner when admiring their hair. "It was a weird way to have control over my destiny" she continued to ramble onto whoever would listen. Every single doll she owned had a fresh haircut and they weren't salon style at all. Her brothers would laugh at her and make her question her motives, but she simply pedaled off with the doll in her basket and showed off to her friends her latest hair creation. She was a more of a tomboy kid, yet also very much a girl. "I tend to yin and yang" she said to herself in meditation. And, she did it all with braided pigtails, lots of hair ribbons in different satiny colors, and matching Mary Jane's on her feet. From the get-go of childhood she was a bona fide feminine girl. The tomboy emerged when the local kids wanted to play kickball and other rough house games and she would join in, wanting to show off that she was good at sports. Yet she was all girly girl, through and through. When the gymnastic pre-teen years gave way to the elementary school drill team and the high school cheerleader years, she was as popular as ever. Her social life was far more important at that age than any book she could even begin to read for her studies. She simply didn't care that much for school. She was more concerned with her uniform and it's required length of skirt (although she managed to alter the length on a weekly basis), the boyfriends' names she etched in marks-a-lot on each saddle shoe, what color cardigan would match her socks, and whether or not to wash her hair, leave it down or put it up in knotted pigtails. Sometimes she would wear a colored bandanna because she didn't feel like washing her hair, especially if the boys weren't coming to visit her school that day, much to the chagrin of the nuns. She always had a fashion dilemma prior to the 8 a.m. school bell, yet wearing uniforms was supposed to be the easiest part of going to a Catholic school. "I'll never have to worry about what to wear" was the common phrase amongst her classmates and friends. As it turns out, most of her best pals always worried about what they wore. As seniors in high school they were allowed to mix and match certain red, whites, and blues within the uniform. Most times her best friends would compare with each other on who had the best looking uniform put together each day. Seniors had advantages, and whenever she wore her navy blue cotton button down, most others followed suit. "It just looked cool" she would tell others as one of the rebels of the class. No teacher or student felt that she studied at all and they were accurate. She simply didn't apply herself in that way. She loved all the physical education classes that were conducted outside, but when it came to books, not so much. She looked onward to college and better days ahead with her choice in fashion.

Autumn in her newly adopted college city was not a typical season. The milder climate of this southern area of the country was more akin to the tropics, which she never minded. But she did miss the four seasons each year. Getting older was okay, as long she didn't have to deal with the snow, ice, and super cold weather that she left behind along with her marriage. Now she was free to wear flip-flops all day, have pretty toes for all to see, and not wear a uniform, thankfully. But, it was one early fall day, where Rachel was itchy to go for a walk to gain a bit more creative inspiration. With the lower humidity and cooler temperatures, she was feeling energetic and bouncy and almost childlike. Something was stirring in her gut and now that she was wiser and more in tune, she paid attention. She looked in the mirror and threw caution to the wind. "Why not?" she asked herself while squinting to part her hair. She then twisted her somewhat longer adult curly hair into interesting messy pigtails. She was also hoping that on this autumn day no one would see her. She just felt like being a silly kid for a moment. She gave into it and walked down the street in flip flops, pigtails, and a big gigantic smile. Because she was almost too proud of her health in these later years, she didn't truly look her age, as she was told. "So what if I wear pigtails with a discombobulated part in the back of my head? Does anyone out here driving on the road really care what I look like? Do they even know me?" these were all the thoughts racing through her brain, as she sauntered down the rock pathway near her small sublet. She was that child again, if only for an hour and a day. Pigtails and all, her heart was brimming with gladness and giddiness on the possibilities of everything. "It's amazing to me that if I fix my hair a certain way, how my body responds to it" the shallowness of her thoughts felt. But she had a point and a purpose and a reason, and pigtails were the expression she chose.

The days were getting shorter, the morning birds not chirping for hours until sunrise, and the evening dusk hours came way too fast. During the carefree summer months, she would wake up with the sunrise and go to sleep after sundown. Now that she was responsibly taking part in a structured job of sorts she had to be at work at a certain time, which meant waking up to an alarm clock at ungodly hours. She abhorred alarm clocks. "So unnatural" she thought, and mentioned to one too many people. Her body wasn't accustomed to being alert when the sun hadn't opened up through the cracks of her blinds, or the wildlife wasn't scampering about the outdoors. She didn't even hear the early dawn trash trucks or nearby highway traffic. "Getting up early to go to work sucks" she thought as she stumbled her way in the darkness to the bathroom to take a look in the mirror at last night's damage. She wasn't a partier, by any means, but at her age, rising so early meant bags and dark circles under each eye, a slow-moving body, hair that had no rhyme or reason, and skin that took on the wrinkles of her pillow case. She was a sight for sore eyes in the mornings, yet she slogged her way through her morning routine of yoga, meditation, tea, and as much creative writing she could muster with a foggy brain before her structured work hours. She was a sound sleeper, but on this particular night, she tossed and turned and reminisced of her fond childhood memories. All of her dreams had images of days and years gone by, and she somehow wished she could time travel back to that bicycle with the doll in the basket. She had no responsibility then, other than to figure out how she wanted to style her dolls' hair, what clothes she wanted them (and herself) to parade around in the neighborhood, and how much she couldn't wait to get home from school to play. Her pigtails were always in full force, and on this morning, when she checked out her image as a fifty-three year old woman, she laughed that she actually had the guts to walk around her current neighborhood with her hair done up in adult pigtails. "I can be so silly sometimes" was her morning mantra on this day. Her childhood was over, her memories were intact, yet she had some bigger fish to fry today. Not only did she have to punch a clock, but she had to deal with some big girl issues and put on her big girl pants. Her complicated mess of a relationship had reared its ugly head in her heart and mind, and she was finally determined to deal with it. She didn't sleep that soundly, her conscience speaking to her in a light slumber because today was the day she had to face the music, be true to herself, be nice with her words and actions, stay on her path, tell the truth, show up for her life, pay attention to everything inside and out, and stay open to the outcome with a detached attitude. She had some work to do, and it didn't involve punching a clock.

It's Complicated

The farthest thing from Rachel's mind was drama. Every morning when she logged into her social networking account, she was reminded and grateful of how simple her life truly had become since her divorces. It's not that each divorce was bitter or ugly or a financial quagmire of sorts, it was that being left to her own devices had her scared, abandoned, and completely unaware of her next move. She had been in relationships and partnerships her entire life, and this time she needed to learn how to be alone and not depend on anyone for anything. She had to grow up. She never imagined that the last many years of her growth stage would involve so many twists and turns through a maze of confusion and struggle. When she was first slapped with divorce papers, which came out of the blue, she was sad and angry. Over time those emotions gave way to freedom and liberation. Then she was on a roller coaster back to sadness and grief and just being pissed off that she wasn't prepared for all of it. She had no one to blame but herself. She was on a lesson of life. When she met this new man, William Jameson, who was a bit younger than she, and seemingly attractive and friendly enough to go out with for a few dates, she wasn't all that interested in becoming emotionally involved with a man at this point in her life, yet having a male friend seemed like a good idea. Someone to bounce ideas off of, especially related to intimacy and the male ego, although she felt she had so much inner work to do that a man would simply interfere. But, he was a nice enough man to enjoy daily talks with, go to bookstores with, and just hang out at coffee shops. "How did I fall for this man now, who is completely the opposite of where my life was and needed to go?" she mused as she stood on her feet all day at her new structured job. "All my energy seems to be directed towards him, who is never going to leave his wife!" was yet another wave of emotion she felt as she helped customers pick out vitamins for their list of ailments. This latest, and her only long term relationship since her divorce was utterly new to her. She had never dated a married man. She never even knew he was married when they first met. He had no ring, never mentioned a wife, barely acted like he was taken, and the topic never came up. "Hmmm, but he doesn't give me details on where he lives and what his situation is all about" she discussed with a friend at her local health club as they sat in the sauna. She wondered if all men who were unhappy in their marriages failed to don a wedding band on their ring finger in the hopes of snaring some sweet naïve soul, such as herself. "Well, it worked, because it's been one whole year later, and he is nowhere near his divorce than when we first met" was her complaint to the receptionist at the health club, who seemed to take an interest in Rachel's love life, as she gave her yet another towel for her sweaty sauna self. The signs were always on the wall, yet she chose to ignore them, and keep her rose-colored glasses on. She was a bit of a dreamer anyway and when it came to relationships any man who possessed authenticity, an incredible gift of gab, intelligence, humor, dressed nicely, had good teeth, strong hands, engaging eyes, and a sense of confidence; just drew her in like bees to honey.

For the next many months of texting and emailing and phone calls, she was in a whirlwind of dating a younger man. She would even boast to her peers who were married to older men, or involved with same-age men, that their sex lives were nowhere near the romantic and sensual romps that Rachel and William had on a daily basis. In a weird sort of way he even helped her overcome her fears of having sex with the lights on. She never quite felt comfortable with her body in her younger years, and with the onset of menopause symptoms, she sure as hell didn't feel that beautiful like she did when they met a year ago. But he always told her just how beautiful he thought she was, and he said it often. As if that didn't make her feel even guiltier about dating a married man, he would have to throw in affirmations on their togetherness. With a daily ritual of yoga, meditation, energetic morning running sessions, and his constantly telling her she was the best thing that ever happened to him, her sense of confidence was back and she felt that her body was better than it was when she was thirty years old. He appreciated every inch of her being and he showed her in ways that would make Penthouse magazine want their sex life for a cover story. She was intimately alive and awake, yet being with a younger complicated lover who wasn't emotionally available at all, made her squirm just a bit. In the beginning this was fine with her, as she wasn't ready or desirous of an emotional connection with a man. Her heart had not completely recovered from the divorce, and her knowing herself, it took a good long while before she could give it away again. He was aware of this and just enjoyed showering her with his affection. "He's probably lacking in any emotional support at home, or his wife doesn't want to have sex with him regularly" was her guilty conscience talking on a daily basis since she became intimately involved with him. Rachel knew about infidelity. She had been on both the giving and receiving end of the destructive force called "cheating". Both times she was heavily involved with relationships that were never quite satisfied with their love lives. Her insecurity and doubt would always surface and she would end up in bed with someone she never thought would go beyond the one-night stand stage. One of these men became her husband, and even though it was longer than she felt necessary to be married to him, since he was her rebound guy from the previous relationship, he did cheat on her and yet she chose to remain loyal. "It's probably best we got divorced, as neither one of us could repress our emotions of feeling trapped" were some words she jotted down in her journal that evening. She was always purging thoughts of past loves and woes and writing did help her move on and maintain some sense of clarity and peace. The best part of William was his willingness to be a good friend and an excellent lover. When they first met she always had butterflies in her stomach and some sweat beads on her forehead, as he brought out her youthful sexy side that was buried for a long time. She didn't want to be so vulnerable right now, but he drew it out of her.

They were inseparable for months. Between constant chats on email, phone calls, and rendezvous during work hours, she was in karma sutra heaven. She all but completely forgot his marital status and just went with the flow of how she was feeling. She never met his wife, yet caught a glimpse of her when William and his legal partner were grocery shopping one Sunday afternoon. She was surprised to see them out and about, and wondered if he even mentioned their budding relationship to any of his friends. Her gut was on overdrive and she started to sincerely feel like the "other woman", and this made her sick to her stomach. She had been there, on the other end, as the wife. It didn't feel good. As she watched him and his wife stroll with the cart out to the parking lot to load their groceries in their car, she hid behind the plant section out in front of the grocery store. "What perfect timing for me to see what she looks like, if they look good together, and why he is going after me" she whispered to the nearest potted plant she was crouching behind, as if the plant was a therapist. She felt that if he caught sight of her he might think she was stalking him, and that was the last thought on her mind, as her heart skipped a few sad beats about his marital status. "Is he ever going to get a divorce, or am I just a fling?" she continued to speak faintly to the large potted array of rose bushes in front of the grocery store, as she clearly wanted to remain out of sight. Many grocery patrons, who were passing by and noticing her unusual stance, brushed it off as yet another crazy bag lady talking to plants. She was always considered one of a kind. She never hid who she was, and on this particular Sunday at the grocery store, life's lessons were speaking volumes to her. William, who was now her lover on a daily basis, was married, was involved with his wife on a domestic level, and probably talked about work and finances at night. "Sheesh, how did I get myself so tangled up in this mess?" she said in a normal tone talking to the sky, as she walked her grocery earth bags to her car, now that he and his wife had driven away. "I'm the other woman!" she literally screamed in her little rolling olive Fiat, hoping that her younger lover was clearly out of the parking lot and on his way back to his married life.

Days and days of the complicated mess of a relationship would wreak emotional havoc on her sleep and daily routine. She thought of him all the time when they weren't together. She missed his body, his smell, his humble ways, his laugh, his touch, and even his constant talk of analytical topics. She tried to rationalize that not being together would keep her integrity intact, yet every day that went by, she wanted to imagine that they were the ones married, instead of his real-time wife. Since she never knew the woman, she could only guess that the wife never knew about the affair. He would call her on his way home from work, he would plan outings for them around his married routine life, and when she left town to visit a friend, he would call her and make sure that the relationship was still functioning on an okay level. It was all so unsettling for Rachel, yet she was caught up in the whole mess for many months. It wasn't the typical relationship she had envisioned post-divorce, but she was definitely enjoying the attention given to her by a younger man. He wasn't that much younger, maybe nine or ten years, but it was enough to make her feel wanted and alive. She tried to change her tack every single time they were together, so he would see that a life with Rachel was far more interesting and exciting than a nine-year emotionally void marriage. Every attempt at conversation, setting examples through her actions, cooking for him when they had a secret moment together, grabbing a frozen yogurt late into the evenings when his wife was at some corporate conference gathering, she was sure he was just as enchanted and wanting the same life as she had wanted for them. "No such luck" she mentioned to her Mom on the phone when asked about her love life. She was always a bit embarrassed to fess up the truth about how he wasn't one day closer to getting a divorce. He even took her to look at apartments one Saturday afternoon, which gave her the feeling that he was going to move out soon and ask her to move in with him. "Far from it" she intimated again to a friend who inquired within. He remained stuck in his complicated life. It probably wasn't such a mess to him, but to her, it was a situation that wasn't going anywhere. She was all ready to change her status on her social networking site months ago, but every time she logged in to update her profile, he would go back home to his married life. It made her sick and tired of dealing with this type of relationship, especially as she envisioned more of a partnership scenario complete with same page activities and mindsets, and zero drama. Now that she was in her premenopausal years, she felt she didn't have to deal with the complication, and simplicity was the only way she chose to live her life. William, his unending marital status, and the drama had to go. "I will feel so much more truthful to myself if I am just strong enough to let go" she peacefully said to herself as she stepped into the shower after a solid hilly run. "He is a good man with a good heart, yet so incredibly slow at making decisions. Do I continue to compromise my well-being, or just cut my losses and run?" she asked herself as she got ready to go to the vitamin job and take care of needy people. She needed to download with a friend. She was so grateful she had many friends who understood her situation and would give her solid and honest advice regarding her younger lover. As complicated as it was, this mess was tough to give up. She never gave up on anything before, but his marital dilemma was far more than what she had signed up for in this lifetime. "Is there a lesson in this for me?" she asked her friend, who was going through a similar situation. All she knew was that she actually felt some peace in the finality of this mess. While she used to constantly check her phone for text messages from him, she was now comfortable in knowing that he had a life elsewhere, and with another woman. The many sleepless nights with thoughts churning in her brain of whether or not they would have a life together was always up for grabs. She would toss and turn and realize that she had indeed fallen for this married man, his serious and critical ways, and how on earth was she going to get out of this mess. Even at her vitamin job she would walk around in a daze and feel as though one day she had it all together, yet the following day she was teetering on the dark side of their ill-fated relationship. "I keep thinking I'm over him, knowing that he has an entire life and history with his wife, but I am so comfortable with him, we have amazing sexual chemistry, and surely that is enough to leave your wife!" she would tell an imaginary dog companion over and over again. She hadn't owned a dog in over a year, when her beloved Labrador died of an unexpected ailment, which left her in a cesspool of amazing grief. Now, being in such a complicated relationship with a married man, who she was sure was solid in breaking up with him, she wished her Labrador dog was by her side to console her during this confusing time. One day she would be all good; the next, her grief sunk her to limitless depths. Due to her change-of-life symptoms that waffled between good days and bad, her mood could turn on a dime to seriously sad and depressed. But all the deep inner soul work that she had embarked upon a few years back gave her solace in knowing that she could endure heartache, have the confidence to move forward without her younger lover, and possibly meet some man who was more in line with her beliefs, was ready and emotionally available, and who was clearly out of any recent previous marriage. Something about married men and not finishing up their business with old relationships always baffled Rachel. She never knew whether it was a sensitive subject to approach on a first date, but after this year with the young married man, she wasn't going to fall prey to any behavior that gave her gut major red flags from the onset. She was good to go on her decision to end the complicated mess with William Jameson. "I can do it. I can do it," she told herself as she posed in front of the mirror, flexed her arm muscles searching for bulging veins that meant she had low body fat, and realized she didn't look so bad after all. She was at peace with her decision and life was ready to flow again as a single woman. "Damn" she thought confidently, and in true Rachel fashion, she empathically gave her blessing to William and went about life in a newfound way.

Vacation in the Jungle

Several weeks had passed, turning into months, and she was well on her way to singlehood bliss. She didn't even consider it being single, as much as leading the life she always wanted to live-her way. She had difficulty taking directions from others; that's why the structured vitamin job, and many other jobs beforehand, had always given her a sense of boredom, restlessness, and rebellion. She was no doubt grateful to have a steady paycheck until her writing royalties came rolling in, and hanging on to the vitamin job provided those much-needed necessities like groceries, gas for the olive, and rent. She was a full-time writer now, and putting that vocation first felt like an accomplishment to her. She didn't have to take orders from anyone anymore, or so her rebellious mind kept telling her. She had the intention out there that she could quit the vitamin job to pursue her passions, or so she kept telling herself and the Universe and planned her life as though all this was already taking place. Her days were full of everything she wanted and needed to do to maintain peace and harmony in her life. She would wake up, apply the necessary essential oils to her specific chakras while sitting on the toilet to her specific chakras, make her green tea, take a few well-earned deep breaths, meditate, do her home yoga makeshift routine, take off on a run, then settle into her gloppy old chair with the laptop for hours writing to her hearts' content. She always had a creative spirit and motivation during the oddest hours of the day. Oftentimes, she would wake up at the wee hours of the morning if she had an inspiring thought, or remembered her dream, and write about it while standing in the kitchen. She would research it. She was curious. She wanted to know what made her tick and why. She was delving even deeper into her soul. After an entire year of being in a complicated mess of a relationship that sucked much of her energy, without her even knowing it, she was now free to take a vacation whenever she felt like it. She had a few ideas, but she had to consult with her bank account to see how far she could go on her freelance writing funds. They hadn't paid off as well as she had liked just yet, but she knew she was set to explode into the writing world with a piece of art so big, that even Ernest Hemingway devotees would be proud. "I feel like all of this hard work I've put in day to day will pay off very soon" she told her Mom, who was always concerned about Rachel's welfare. She would reassure her mother that she was one step away from being a successful writer. She even sent her Mom recently released published articles, to give her some peace of mind. There was never any strong male presence in her life growing up, so the survival skills she adopted as a young child were all she knew.

Despite her efforts to be productive after the fallout of her younger man, she needed a break. It wasn't so much that there had been drama, quite the opposite. She had professed over and over again to her young lover that they couldn't go any farther unless he chose a different path. She wasn't necessarily giving him an ultimatum or wanted to change him, but she did want him to disentangle himself from his wife prior to furthering their relationship. "Oh well, I did the best I could" were her thoughts on a day-by-day basis, as she began to feel freedom. Nonetheless, the very thought of taking a vacation and changing her routine excited Rachel. She would Google map locations for a possible road trip; she would check all the various airline discount sites and plug in imaginary cities she could travel to, if she had the money. She went so far as to manifest a vacation through new moon rituals and asking her friends to put it out there every time the planets and stars were lined up accordingly. She got lucky one day. There was a tremendous discount on a round trip flight to Central America, where an old soul sister spent some quality time at the beach in a foreign country to further her education in healing and wellness. They had always talked about reconnecting at some point, yet Rachel never thought it would be in another country. But this offer online was way too tempting and she punched in all the correct information, secured the flight, then her body began to feel all the impulses of spontaneity. Her newfound self was preparing for a trip overseas, and from her newly adopted college city location, it wasn't all that far. Approximately four hours on an airplane and she would be reunited with her dear friend, and engaging in the culture of another country. Nicaragua wasn't even on her radar, but the beach, the sun, the ocean, nature, and a peaceful environment, and she felt good to go. She was all set to take off in about a month.

Every day at her structured job she thought about this upcoming trip to Nicaragua. She talked about it with coworkers, she gazed out the window and envisioned what it would be like, and sometimes she even needed validation that she was doing the right thing. Whenever she checked her bank account, she would look to the heavens and pray that there would be a miraculous bump in her bottom line. This caused her some worry, but not enough to cancel the trip, forego seeing her soul sister who she had missed for four years, and experiencing a new and unique place. Her friend had mentioned Nicaragua many times in months past, but Rachel wasn't ready to take the plunge. Now that she was a free woman and no longer involved in a complicated relationship, she was more than ready for the trip.

She always packed light. She knew from previous experiences the more she carried, the more she would lose along the way, never wear half the clothes she brought, and would always end up leaving some shampoo or big bottle of lotion behind, simply because it was too heavy and wouldn't make the 3 oz. cut through security. She hadn't traveled that much overseas, but she did have a great sense of wisdom about practicality when it came to paring her stuff down to a minimalist status. Packing her suitcase was just another indication that her common sense had indeed surfaced, despite all the previous unsettledness about her life. This trip to Nicaragua needed a passport and cash. She would be able to do a money exchange when she arrived in Central America, as she wasn't the least bit worried about her pocketbook. She had heard about the rampant theft in the area, but she was staying with her soul sister, Rebecca, who was wary enough for the both of them. Rachel didn't require that much food or outings, she wasn't planning to purchase any trinkets, and she sure as hell didn't need a pedicure. The trip was bare bones to the core. She packed just one small bag, her laptop for writing and staying in touch with some friends and family, and about three pairs of flip flops. She was traveling to a foreign country with a great deal of confidence and no worry. She had not felt this way in so many years and she attributes the feeling to all the lessons she had learned through divorce, taking care of her own financial needs, making big girl decisions about her livelihood, and being older and smarter. That's not to say that she didn't have a wild streak, which she nurtured quite a bit, but it was always her soul talking that did the crazy things. At least her friends and family felt they were crazy moves and actions. To Rachel her irresponsible behavior was all part of her soul and what it needed. She felt she began to break rules at an early age-in the era of sex, drugs, and rock and roll-so anything weird beyond that point was all part of her DNA. She knew this about herself and would never deny what her intuition and gut were saying. This time her inner being wanted her to travel to Nicaragua for two weeks, relax, recharge, do something different, be a part of a new culture, meet foreign people, and see her old soul sister once again.

Flying into Nicaragua was a bit of an experience for her. She passed through security, as her passport was up to date, her suitcase was small enough to forego any extra fees, and she didn't set off the alarm with any unusual clothing accessories or sharp implements in her bag. "Mission accomplished" she said smiling while passing the TSA agent. This leg of the trip was cake for her. The flight itself was only four hours and she was able to fall asleep rather quickly, as the early morning shuttle bought her some much-needed sleep time to the airport. She always slept on flights. Even the small commuters to not-so-distant cities she would nestle into the uncomfortable and rigid seats, use a rolled up blanket (if she could ever locate one on the plane) or an old plastic water bottle to slide behind her lower back and help her posture. "The airplane seats are so unforgiving" she leaned over and mentioned to the dude sitting next to her giving her an offbeat stare. Finding a pillow to rest her head was another task altogether. She would often wad up a piece of clothing from her backpack, and if that wasn't available, she would coil her arm underneath her neck as a pillow. Either way, she was always terribly uncomfortable on airplanes. Airline travel certainly had its drawbacks, least of all comfort and a decent meal. She always brought along her trail mix, a piece of fruit, always passing on the small, processed, plastic-tasting food the airline always managed to serve. "It amazes me that they can still charge so much for a flight to anywhere in Timbuktu, you'd think they would make your travel more comfortable. Even peanuts are a pastime on these planes," she would say to weird staring dude, or to any nearby traveling person stuffed into a seat around or next to her. She never wanted to actually start a conversation with anyone on an airplane. She just wanted to sleep in contorted positions and wake up when the plane landed. On the first leg of the flight to Houston there were many people traveling to various cities, and in an effort to save money on the flight, she chose one with about three different layovers for many hours in each city. It wasn't always her best choice, but when it came to her bottom line, she did have a slight sense of practicality and realism. "Heaven forbid I have to depend on anyone to foot my bills" she opened her eyes to say to the fake small reading light above.

The plane landed in Houston, a big city full of big people, and she was wishing she could just go for a run and show them how it's done. Everyone at this airport wore Wrangler jeans, big cowboy hats, donned big bellies, was waiting in line for fast food at the gazillion eateries, businessmen glued to their cell phones, and just a million people going in twelve thousand different directions. It made her a bit dizzy as she stopped, recited the serenity prayer to herself and wormed her way into a food line to grab a small green something to eat. She had more peace in her heart and soul than ever before, but not much compassion for large people who could be responsible and help themselves not be so big. "Don't they notice in the mirror when their pants are increasing in size? I mean, seriously!" were her thoughts drifting to the salad section no one was particularly interested in during airport rush hour. She kept telling herself how extremely grateful she felt for this process called "life", despite having to slog her way through one job or another, in an effort to fulfill her vocation and passion. She was bound and determined to do it. She knew that hard work and perseverance were the backbone of any goal. She was also aware of the many years it took her to get where she was and she wasn't about to let silly fears or boundary-less big people stand in her way. She felt it was all about timing and luck. Her level of inner contentment was at an all-time high. "For every action, there is a reaction" was the mantra of a close friend of hers, who injected that statement every time she was about to take another adventure in life. "All is well" was Rachel's response to her friend silently hinting that she was more than okay.

Most of her friends were eclectic, wise, loving, and driven. Over the years she had weeded out those friends who no longer served a purpose in her life. She felt it wasn't such an awful tragedy to align herself with people and connections who fed her soul. Being in her 50s she felt that those who remained loyal, honest, and true, were the close friends whom she cherished. Not a day, month, or year went by where she didn't show her appreciation for the friends in her life. Whether by email or phone or in-person visits, she made sure her friends knew how special they were. It was the Rachel that the Universe wanted all along. "I feel my destiny is to be where I'm needed, here, there, and everywhere!" was her demanding conscience telling her on a daily basis. She was willing to travel to places with limited funds, simply to reconnect, have some fun, shine some light, and share her wisdom and self with those who knew her best. Most times she would welcome the opportunity to meet several new people, to gain an understanding of others' viewpoints and how the world works. Whether they remained close friends forever, which was never the question. It was the connection that felt special to her. Some people stayed, others simply faded away. Friendship, to her, was priceless and limitless. She was now on her way to Nicaragua to visit Rebecca, one of her dearest soul sisters, who she hasn't seen in four years. And her heart was wide open and begging for a change.

The big airbus landed in the main city of Managua. Her adventures were just beginning, but exactly how it all looked remained somewhat of a mystery, she felt. She knew she had to get to one certain little beach city, but navigating to this remote area was more than her brain could logically process, and she had a tinge of fear as to what to do next. She was to board a small puddle jumper plane that seated only eight passengers and travel to the southernmost tip of the country on a beautiful and remote beach area. "How do I know which taxi to take?" "Do I even take a taxi?" "Can I communicate the language with the locals, and oh my God, what did I just do?" said her crazy spinning thoughts as she searched for the airline puddle jumper. It was a tiny plane compared to the luxury 747 she had just deplaned. She thought about her motion sickness issues "but ginger and I are best friends, so I'm good" she casually told a fellow future tiny plane passenger. She went through the usual routine of bag check, pat downs, shoes off through security, and whatnot, only there were no big people. Nicaragua had lean, sinewy types. "It's amazing to me that even in this country and boarding such a small plane, I have to go through this routine all over again." Her rebellious side was rearing its ugly head. Yet, rules were rules, and she reluctantly abided by them. "Just this time," she strongly told her conscience. She was in foreign country now and she never knew what was going to happen at any given moment. She had traveled to foreign countries before in her past, even before her marriage; but this trip felt different in somehow, as if she knew something was going to happen in a good way. Not only seeing her good friend, but a general sense that her life will be different after the 10 days. She wrote furiously in her journal every chance she had, documenting her feelings and the changes taking place in the course of her days. It gave her the impetus to feel creative and inspired, even on those days where her writing seemed to be stuck in muck. She felt a surge of energy and motivation to write at the oddest times, at dawn, while in the shower, on a run, driving to the grocery store, it consumed her. She wrote all the time now.

As the puddle jumper took off she was seated next to a young couple on their way to their honeymoon destination. Both of them had never been in another country outside the United States, much less an airplane as small as this one, so the husband was feeling a bit queasy. He was slumped over most of the flight with his head between his legs in his lap while the young bride rubbed his back. Rachel felt empathy for them. She had her own past years of motion sickness on all modes of transportation, from riding in back seats of cars, to sailboats on a rocky ocean ride, to amusement parks' roller coasters, to bus rides, train rides, and of course, airplanes. The feeling as though she was going to vomit was always in full swing. The young honeymooning couple had her utmost in sympathy. It was only a short flight-about 30 minutes-yet the pilots' altitude was very low and the propellers on the planes' wings churned around furiously as the pilot talked to his copilot the entire time about everything but flying the plane. With the ocean only miles down below, she was a bit comforted by the fact she was a good swimmer. If there was ever a time to crash, this was it. As comfortable as she was, the young honeymooners were not so fortunate. The groom looked over at Rachel and asked her if this was her first time on such a plane. "Actually, no" she said to the young pale man, who looked as if he could hurl at any moment. "I have flown a few times in similar conditions, but I too, would feel exactly how you are feeling at this moment" she claimed sympathetically to the sick young man. His young bride just stuck her head in the tiny window looking out at the ocean below. She also felt as if they could drop into the ocean at any time if the plane malfunctioned. Land was approaching and Rachel kept reassuring the groom that "we are almost there," even though she had just intimated her newfound knowledge of flying in prop planes, the ride was rough, and her gut wasn't feeling all that great. It did land safely, and the young honeymooners were well on their way to a week of bliss in a foreign country. She wished them well, yet the sickly groom couldn't even walk straight, much less wrap his arms around his new bride.

The airport was nothing more than a thin landing strip, one small desk, two attendants to check all bags, someone positioned to take more money from travelers for an "airport" fee, and many taxis waiting to take passengers to their destination. She was running out of Nicaraguan money and had to get to an ATM to withdraw some more funds and do the money exchange thing. The question on her mind was "where do I go from here?" She had arrived on the peninsula, but wasn't sure exactly where Rebecca lived. They never quite discussed the particulars. Nicaragua doesn't have regular American street names, so she was perplexed as to what to tell a taxi driver. "Drive to Rebecca's house" she laughed at herself while trying to figure out which taxi driver would give her the best deal. She got lucky. There was a driver holding a sign with her name on it. He was standing in front of an old red Pathfinder, a big smile on his face, and looking extremely happy knowing he would make an American tip that day. She drained most of her money after the ATM visit, but she would give him whatever she had that felt worth the drive he was about to make. "Who told this driver to pick me up?" she asked herself while rolling her small bag towards the local sign holder. Since she was on an adventure it didn't matter. "Who else would be named Rachel Harper in this foreign county?" she surmised after exchanging small broken

English pleasantries with the driver. She then hopped into the passenger seat in front and they drove off down the dusty brown dirt road full of potholes.

She arrived at her destination, for the life of her she had no idea how, but she was "escorted" out of the SUV, small bag and all and shown where Rebecca lived. One thing she learned about being in a foreign country, people were not in a hurry, and everyone seemed to know who everyone was and where they lived. She simply mentioned her friend's name, Rebecca, and she was plopped in the middle of her dirt driveway that led to about four different little casitas about a stone's throw from the ocean. "Wow, she really has such a cool place here, I would never leave," she said to the courteous local driver who was kind enough to forego a tip. Fortunately, Rebecca was rumbling around with dishes in the small and open kitchen and Rachel said her name as she was approaching. Rebecca dropped what she was doing and they hugged each other so hard it would have been tough to pull them apart. Both women had been through the ringer in their lives. Both knew their friendship was a cherished one, and both knew that this trip was a catalyst of some sort. Rebecca was so elated to see her. She knew Rachel was coming, but it had been so long since they hung out, the feeling of deep friendship just welled up inside both of them. Rebecca was a true beach girl now. Gone were the big mountains and big races and big everything that they were both submerged in during a former life. She was now simple, brown as a berry, super fit and trim, and very much a local to the Nicaraguan influence. Rachel was thrilled to see the metamorphosis, and they caught up for hours. After she set down her small bag the two of them set off to take a walk on the beach. It was so unpopulated, vast and energetic. They walked for a long time, feet deep in the sand, and felt as though time apart was never an issue. If anything they picked right back up where they left off from their days in the mountain town. Both Rachel and Rebecca had essentially grown up. Both were simple and willing and ready. Both were truly on paths that seemed to mimic each other, despite their fifteen-year age difference, and both had an adventurous spirit that never went away. She had ten days to soak in every inch of Nicaragua and she was prepared in her mind and body to do just that.

Every morning both women would concoct a very simple breakfast of tea, some organic cereal or maybe an egg, a wealth of pineapple, and top it off with a square or two of dark chocolate. The nourishment seemed to set the tone for the day, which mainly consisted of slathering on tons of sunscreen, the tiniest bikinis ever known to man, and sauntering down to the sand to sit, do some reminiscing, walk some more, dip in the ocean, talk about everything under the sun, and basically plan how their lives were set to evolve. Neither Rachel nor Rebecca were in any hurry at all, as they knew they had many days together to enjoy before each one retreated back to their lives in their respective countries. Just the thought of going back to America made her question many motives about government and why certain American ways were much more hectic and stressful than where she was currently sitting, that being a large colorful beach towel. Rebecca was set to return to the USA as well, as Rachel soon found out, and she was feeling excited, nervous, and a bit apprehensive about leaving a country that she had grown so accustomed to. "Won't you feel like you are reinventing the wheel going back?" she asked, but Rebecca reassured her that she was going to be just fine. Rebecca had new tools to use with old ways of living. Rachel also knew that the next ten days were going to be transformative in a way she had never experienced. It was just her gut going into overdrive. Rebecca planned to leave earlier than expected and Rachel had five whole days of the trip to herself. "Why are you leaving so much sooner than the end of the month?" she asked Rebecca as they turned over on their towels in the sand to make sure they didn't have uneven tan lines. Rebecca said she wanted to return to school, and the entry date was sooner than expected so she had to go back to America and get acclimated to her new/old environment. "Makes perfect sense, but it seems weird for me to be here in Nicaragua while you journey back to the United States," was her casual response when they both were talking timelines for their mutual trips. Rebecca felt a bit badly she decided to leave early and abandon Rachel in a foreign country, but giving her so many close-by contacts for language translation would help her secure a bike for short transportation needs, and possibly ease her way with the foreign Spanish tongue. She mentioned the guy who runs the hotel next door, in case she had some specific problems or needs that one of the other resources were unable to handle, how he was an American transplant and became a good buddy of Rebecca's, so she felt confident giving her the down low on it being okay to ask him for help. "It's always safe to know that there is someone nearby who can speak English and help with any little issues that might crop up," Rebecca said, as if to reassure her own self that Rachel would be okay.

A Random
Meeting

After a few days on her own and feeling rather confident in the foreign country, she felt like exploring a bit more in areas she had no clue about. Rebecca had ventured back to her American mountain home and Rachel was left to her own devices. One afternoon while feeling sort of lost as to what to do without Rebecca, she meandered next door and sought out the man who was to be her American translation savior. He was the hotel manager and everything in between, as Rebecca so eloquently phrased it and Rachel eventually found out. There was a rustling in the kitchen of the beachfront hotel and she meandered towards the ruckus. No one was around during the middle of the afternoon, and most tourists were at the beach or on some zip lining expedition. Either way, her curiosity was high and she felt that her remaining five days deserved some adventure. And who best to give it than the man next door, who Rebecca had recommended. When she approached the kitchen she was baffled and almost giddy to see a man playing around on the kitchen floor with a sweet brown dog. He, too, was shocked to see someone as pretty as Rachel. Their eyes met they had some interesting connection that they couldn't quite define, and they began to talk incessantly about everything. He was a bit nervous, as was she, but it quickly dissipated with the ongoing words they exchanged. Soon they became fast friends. It was as if there was never a moment where they weren't friends. She thought it was so weird that she could connect with a man so fast, but after years of deep inner work nothing was completely out of the ordinary. They talked and talked and talked, for hours. She couldn't remember the last time she felt so comfortable and full of so many words, it felt as though she couldn't get enough said in each minute that passed by. They didn't even sit down to talk; just stayed in the kitchen and let the world sort of pass them by. This interesting and curious man, whose name was Jonathan, didn't leave any stone unturned. He preferred to be called his entire name, versus some abbreviation like "Jon," which he always felt made him out to be a hairdresser or wannabe actor. "Say my entire name when addressing me, and I'm a happy man" he said with a strong affirmation. They continued the conversation for another few moments wondering what it was she came over to his hotel in the first place. "Was I going to ask Jonathan something about directions, or local banks, or a decent grocery store?" "I can't seem to remember the nature of why I'm here" her thoughts drifted for a moment while watching him continue to wrestle with the cute dog. That alone caught her attention, his ability to be with dogs and just go with the flow. Dogs were roaming all around the small beach community and she couldn't wait to be part of it in more depth, now that he was on the scene and a possible tour guide.

The two of them left the kitchen, still continuing to talk about books, travel, family, recent encounters with friends from distant places, filling all the void conversation spaces with "sighs" and "uh huhs". What struck her as so familiar was their mutual love of writing and adventure. The way he spoke was like poetry to her. She was never a great fan of poetry, but she did appreciate eloquence in dialogue by any man. Intelligence was also very high on her list of manly qualities she appreciated and desired in a partner. He too, was admiring of her words, as they both seemed to know instinctively what the other was saying. "Here I am in a foreign country and I run into a man who seems to know everything I'm feeling from the get-go. How odd is that?" was her heart now speaking. She was a believer in synchronicity and serendipitous meetings, yet she wasn't completely sure that this encounter with him was anything like that. "Or was it?" said her racing mind. After so many years of wrenching heartaches and relieved of their entanglements, she finally met a man who could be a potential friend for life. She didn't want to put the cart before the horse, but she also didn't want to banish the thought that this chance meeting with him was way too odd for any explanation. It wasn't like any man she had met in America; like those uncomfortable grocery store run-ins, the concert gatherings where they would bump into each other at the bar while ordering a drink, or the casual "hey there" while passing one another on a run around the lake. The new man in the foreign country was vastly different.

In the past and during the course of her marriage unfolding into a drama-ridden coupling, she began to read anything and everything related to spirituality and how to become a better person, a more grounded and heart-centered individual, and to be content. This included following a path of her soul. How her soul was to be in this world, who she was, and what the Universe had wanted for her, was her new calling. She studied for endless hours on the topic. She attended community gatherings where everyone in the room shared their story and felt compassion for one another. She started drifting away from friends who were no longer in alignment with her newfound beliefs. She simplified her life. She restructured her priorities and became more responsible. Every book topic she read was about soul mates and twin flames and karmic meetings. She would walk everywhere she could, dogs in tow with the hopes they would be accepted in outdoor cafes and bookstores. It was there she felt compelled to study, read, and desired solitude. Fortunately, she had lived in a mountain town where dogs were accepted everywhere, and she had three well-behaved loyal canines, who became known throughout the community. She was always so grateful when her dogs were welcomed at all places. She even went so far as to take them into the small chapel where she sat every week for a few hours at a time, lit some candles, and prayed silently that the course of her life would mimic all that she was now reading and studying. Her dogs simply stayed by her side and absorbed the peace and tranquility of the chapel as much as she did. "Those were the days" she said to a friend on a recent coffee shop conversation about the latest skis and boots. She was no longer interested in skiing, per se, but since she lived in a mountain town that received a fair amount of yearly snow, the topic of skiing and its wardrobe came up from time to time.

She was becoming a very spiritual being, full of radiance and warmth and wisdom. Her closest friends had noticed the shift in her persona and she accredited it to her being so open and accepting of what the Universe was putting on her path. With almost three long years of being on a soulful journey, she was well aware of others who shared the same belief and feeling.

After being in Nicaragua for such a short amount of time, she had already felt that something was different. It wasn't so much where she was, but the very depth of her soul yearning for what it needed.

Jonathan's Story

When they sat down for hours on the beach, initially Rachel was intrigued by Jonathan's being and what he was all about. She wanted to hear more about how he landed where he did, how he managed to stay in one place for so long with no American amenities, and why on earth was he still single. Since he liked to talk, he managed to chew her ear off with his story. She listened intently, but in her usual manner, her mind drifted off to the ocean's waves and the birds flying above, waiting for a green flash to happen over the sea during sunset, but he continued to tell his story.

"I was born in the south. My wife and I had transplanted to this Central American country way back in the early 90s. We both had corporate cubicle jobs, desires to seek more adventure and freedom, and she wanted a child. With both of our retirement accounts we sought to purchase a sailboat and travel to distant lands. Neither one of us knew what or where we wanted to go, but the calling of somewhere different was imminent, so as soon as we delivered our notices to our respective jobs, we hit the high seas." Rachel sat in the sand listening the best she could, but she kept having weird thoughts as to why he felt the need to share his story. She thought perhaps this unloading of his story would be his own cathartic experience, as not many in his near vicinity could speak English. She was just the person that Jonathan needed to tell his story to, as he could sense her overall lack of judgment on humanity. "I was an accomplished sailor, after many years of living near the eastern coast of North Carolina. I grew up in a small rural neighborhood, yet always spent the good part of the summers at the Atlantic Ocean. I had befriended several local sailors at the restaurants, bars, and piers in the bay. I would pick their brains on how to be a world traveling sailor. Most of the older men who had been around the block a few times, were commercial fisherman. They applauded my enthusiasm but also warned that the disadvantages far outweighed the advantages. Being a fisherman was a lonely job, as most of the men could attest to many afternoons at the local bar. They were always away from their families and friends for weeks and months at a time. Often they would return with nary a catch or a mere pittance compared to their Pacific Ocean competitors. Not that they kept up with the other side of the continent, but a cold water ocean fish was more preferable for the mainlanders, given the growth of bacteria and potential parasites in the warmer waters of the Atlantic. Even the Caribbean had more activity for the commercial fisherman, as the water was cleaner, deeper, and less likely to produce any intestinal issues for regular people unaccustomed to a diet high in seafood."

The sun was beginning to set, she started to shift her gaze from the clouds to Jonathan and back to the wavy ocean. She desperately wanted to see the green flash everyone kept mentioning, yet he couldn't squash his need to share more. "I wasn't interested in becoming a commercial fisherman. I simply wanted to sail and see the world by boat. My wife and I eventually bought a 30-foot sailboat, and I was well on my way to become the traveler and explorer I had hoped would happen. I took the required courses necessary to man the craft and although it tried my patience a few times with technicalities, I was still able to attain my license and sail a boat. Months went by and we put together a plan on when and where we would go first. Departing from the Atlantic meant we would have to travel far south and sail due west, if we were desirous of an adventure to Central or Latin America. If we chose to travel northeast and then west, we would spend greater amounts of time up the Atlantic coast, then venture into the Indian Ocean, and eventually wind up in Japan. That trip alone was a bit daunting for us, so we mapped out the southern and western routes. The waters were warmer and we felt more comfortable venturing around the Caribbean and possibly Cuba."

Jonathan began to feel more comfortable oozing out details of his adventures and woes to Rachel. She was becoming more enthralled with just how passionate he was regarding his arrival into Nicaragua. She tried to not let her attention wander too much, as she sensed he needed to talk even more. "Once we landed here, after months at sea, I was elated at seeing a new country. We both felt that it was home the minute we stepped off the sailboat. Something about the foreign land appealed to us in ways that we couldn't even explain. With a long lost Spanish background, I knew I was on home soil without actually knowing why. It just felt right. We were at peace with our decision, so we anchored the boat close to shore and traversed through the sand and jungle to our newfound paradise. It didn't take long before we finagled our way into the hearts of the locals. I have to say that we had that kind of appeal, and we were welcomed and appreciated." She was bemused that his ego began to rear its head.

"We didn't have much money, just what we withdrew from our life savings in America to embark on this expedition, but it didn't matter. With our new life underway and our desire to live modestly being at the top of the priority list, we chose the most simple way of living, albeit so incredibly different than our home in the old southern suburbia town off the eastern American coast. Beginning a new life in Nicaragua demanded some scaling down, and seeing as we traveled with basically nothing, it wasn't too great a task to hole up in a tiny rented apartment until we figured out our next move. Plus, my wife really wanted a child." His story showed some humility, but it also showed Rachel that she was beginning to be a good listener. "Months went by and the "child" topic came up in random discussions many times; so much so that the pressure on our marriage was starting to show. We decided to sink our energies into buying a piece of land and constructing our own house. With the money we saved and the affordability of the country, it was a highly sought after piece of land that caught our attention. We negotiated in our broken Spanish language, secured the deal after days of back and forth easygoing talks, and we were finally landowners in a foreign country. This all happened after only a few months of citizenship paperwork and finding part time jobs to prove our stability" he continued shaking his head. "It was no longer foreign to me. This was our new home, with no car, no mortgage, no corporate job, no big city life, and no more obligations that America was demanding of us in the worst way. We began to write up plans to build our own house, the way we wanted it to be, using the most native textiles and wood and recycled materials we could find. It was to be a five-year project."

Her head turned to a few stray dogs sauntering by in the sand and he never stopped talking. "As construction took place, with the help of several local hands and tools, I decided I was truly a master woodworker. I hadn't dabbled in that field since my younger days, but the craftsmanship and my abilities came pouring back into this new home construction. My wife began working more and mentioning her need for a child almost every minute of every day. It was tiring for me, as my focus was on building a very nice house for us in the jungle." She could sense he was proud of the amount of sacrifice it took to get to this place, and she thought his story was finished at that moment, but he kept going. She just wanted to see the green flash.

"So that's exactly what I did, yet my wife stewed alone in the construction zone makeshift kitchen. Her moods were becoming extreme with respect to starting a family, and I began to remind her that having a new house was priority before bringing a child into the world. I would appease her with my logic more often than not, but she couldn't help but feel depressed about getting older and not having a baby yet." He started to get a bit teary-eyed at this point of his story, but never missed a detailed beat, and she continued to listen and look out onto the ocean and sunset.

"The waves were crashing down below the job site, the monkeys were howling in the trees, and the geckos were chirping their loud noises every morning. It was the perfect spot for true bliss, and I was grateful and pleased every day of my creation on the hill above the jungle. The home still had amazing 180-degree views of the Pacific and Caribbean seas, and we snapped one photograph after another to send to family and friends back in America. I was proud of my work and it showed. No amount of travel, fear, wife-nagging, and job confusion could deter me from what I felt was my greatest creation. "Why do we need a child, when we just created a pristine quality home in an amazing paradise?" "I feel as though we just gave birth to this project" I would say to her over a simple dinner of local fish and fruit. She was still not convinced that a new home could replace an actual living being created between two people, but she decided to withdraw into her own depressed self and meander around town looking for a hobby to sink her teeth into. I spent my days surfing, chatting with the locals, connecting with all the Nicaraguan businesses, shopping and cooking. I was basically a one-man show, as she kept to herself and kind of sunk more into her depression. As much as I loved her in our former days in America, I was now seeing a different side to her and I wanted to start a new beginning in Nicaragua on a larger-than-life note. Not so much with material items, but how my heart was expanding on a daily basis. It's as if the more I ventured around the town getting to know the ins and outs of living like a local, the more open I was to whatever came onto my path. I was grounding in a way that I never felt in the United States. I was heart-centered and my soul was taking me in directions I never could explain, especially to my wife. When we did interact, which was intermittent at best, I suggested we try going our own way for a bit. She wasn't thrilled with the idea. If anything, it angered her that

I couldn't see how desperate she was to have a family. I only felt pressured and pushed by her words and actions, yet my soul was happily applying the pressure I had wanted and craved for years. I not only discovered a fresh start in island and foreign living, but the newfound beating of my heart and how the blueprint of my soul was taking shape became front and center. I had awakened."

They started to stroll on the beach after the sunset and no green flash had taken place, yet he was sensing her need to move after an hour of his story spilling, almost surprising himself that he could be so open with her. She had that way about her where people just wanted to tell her their story. Jonathan was no different. "After two years of living under the same roof with her that no longer felt love and hope and happiness for anything other than some friends down at the neighborhood surf shop, I moved out. My prestigious home I had built with my own two hands, using native materials and constructed with precision, was now left to my wife and her own whimsical ways. As relieved as I was to not have to deal with her constant barrage of anger and subsequent depression since our arrival into the foreign country, I was thrilled to submerge into my passions of surfing, writing poetry, and hanging out with the local dogs that roamed the beaches. It also led me to one of the best jobs here on the island. Since I have a rather likeable demeanor whom everyone finds somewhat engaging, this beachfront bed and breakfast joint decided to hire me to be their manager." At that moment she got a bit turned off by his ego, but after hearing the so much of his story, she let it go and realized it made up the sum of his parts. "I willingly accepted without hesitation, and thus began my new career in a foreign land.

Gerry Ellen

They even pay me more than I know what to do with, as I am now renting and living in a tiny rancho on stilts, with an open kitchen accessible to the outdoor bugs and jungle creatures, a mattress on the floor in the upstairs, sparse running water in the small shower, a hammock strung from one palm tree to the next for my evening wind down times, and a beat up old motorcycle to help me get around town. I had decided to scale back my living since accepting this new manager job, yet as I recline in the hammock most nights listening to the distant monkeys in the trees, I can't help but imagine what the stars would have looked like from the luxury home I built on the hill overlooking the beach. My wife lives there now, and I finally have contacted my lawyer in America to draw up legal papers, end my marriage of fifteen years, and live life with no care or worries in the world in my newly adopted foreign country." She was surprised that he was so candid with the finale, but she also knew after hearing his words that he was so ready to move on.

The Next Step To Fulfillment

*L*iving life in a foreign country, although very appealing to her, the very thought of existing without her creature comforts made her feel uneasy. She was so accustomed to her morning routine of green tea, quiet meditation, yoga, a run around the hilly neighborhood where she lived, the dogs and cats who she had come to know by name and see on a regular basis, her close-knit group of soul sisters, the vegan lifestyle she had recently adopted, and just a general sense of having some roots. It's been ages since she had roots. "But, I'm always open to what my path has in store for me" was her constant surrender mantra, as she breathed in and out with precision in her makeshift home yoga practice. The recent vacation in the jungle and meeting Jonathan certainly piqued her interest and heart strings, yet there was a feeling of another big event happening in her life. She had completed a pivotal point on her soul's path, and since her divorce, which took all she had to gather up steam and move forward, she felt as though a new part of her soul and life was emerging into the even larger unknown. It excited her although she didn't obsess about it like years before. She listened, she was aware, and she moved about the world in a more mature way than ever before. She even felt responsible and took ownership in mistakes where she knew a lesson was sure to emerge.

As she settled in to her city, with all the devoted college fans, the hippies, the throwbacks from the 70s, the yuppies, the retirees, the techies, and even the devout religious zealots, she had discovered the diversity that is her city. She remained flexible and willing, her ticket to success and contentment. Wherever and whenever she was needed somewhere, she was there in a heartbeat. If a friend was down on her luck, she and her would go for a long walk and talk it out. If one of her distant friends on the west coast needed to download, she would spend hours on the phone listening and offering whatever advice she could muster, which would make her friend feel at ease. If someone who she was connected to via social networking had a crisis, or needed to raise money for some charity that she believed in, she never hesitated to make the person feel as though they were important. The internet and social marketing had a way of giving her a sense of purpose, even with thousands of miles separating their paths. She was most at home when visiting friends in other cities and countries. She was also exploring a new friendship with Jonathan in Nicaragua. "A very deep friendship" she thought many times over, not only in her head, but in her heart and soul.

After her return from Central America they would stay in touch about every day. Whether through email or an occasional phone call, they managed to continue a close friendship. It intrigued her due to the nature of it all. The soul connection, the literary companionship, the love of nature and animals, and his way of talking, gave her this peaceful feeling. Oftentimes, he spoke way too much, professing to know quite a bit and speaking as if he were some Tao giving a sermon on top of a mountain. She could listen for about a half hour, try to get a word in edgewise, and eventually give up and continue to listen. He repeated himself quite a bit, and this tired her, which led her to screen his calls more often than not. What really bothered her was she felt she couldn't tell him how she would get cauliflower ear every time they talked on the phone for well over an hour. She didn't mind hearing him live and in person telling his story, but the phone was another matter altogether. Granted, it had been weeks since they spoke, but going over the same conversation and topics left her with a sense that nothing new had transpired in Nicaragua, and what could possibly call her back there. If they were on similar soul paths, she felt he needed to explore more of his own blueprint. "It took me a good three years to travel, live simply, make mistakes, learn lessons, and pick myself up before I knew my soul completion with my past had transpired" she said to a girlfriend in a recent email Rachel wasn't entirely sure that Jonathan had taken the steps to move forward in his soul. "Soul work is tough work" she told her friend. "It's not something to be taken lightly." "It needs to be honored and made aware of on a daily basis." "Was he hiding his own soul's needs behind a mirage of Buddhism and surfing and his continued life with his son and ex-wife?" This was a thought that permeated her mind quite a bit, especially since she was fantasizing that they could possibly grow a life together. She was in no hurry. She wasn't even sure it was the right path, but it intrigued her. She definitely was on an open path of who knows what, living life with purpose and love each and every day. It was what she felt in her heart. She had finally chosen to be true to herself.

The friendship with him was far too important for her to let it slide into oblivion. On a recent holiday trip back to California visiting family and friends, she had this feeling that something was amiss. She hadn't heard from him in over a week. No daily email, no beautiful scenic nature photos sent to her inbox, no phone calls. "What is up?" she thought to herself on the flight to California. Granted, she was moving very slowly with this newfound friendship. Given her recent complications with William in the college city, which took her months to get over, she wanted to honor the path of her soul. She needed to use patience and timing to return to Nicaragua, if at all, and perhaps begin some sort of existence with another man, who she still wasn't clear on the purpose.

He wasn't patient, as he had proclaimed. She would offer new information regarding him to many of her friends. They weren't convinced that they were meant for each other. Something felt off. Her friends commented, she felt it, and she trusted her gut to take it one step at a time. On a clear starry evening, when she visited Annabelle, an old friend from San Francisco, they returned to Annabelle's townhome after an outing of pedicures and strolls in the park to chat, she opened her email to find a letter from him. Her gut sank, but in the "I-just-lost-a-friend-who-bared-his-soul-with-me" kind of way. It wasn't the typical boyfriend/girlfriend feeling of love lost. It wasn't as though her heart was no longer on fire. It was different, and she couldn't explain it. She couldn't believe what she was reading. He claims he had soul-searched in the past week and had met someone else rather abruptly. Since he was in the high season at his hotel, one of his guests piqued his interest and charm. His words to her in the email were thoughtful and true, and so unexpected. She was just readying herself for what would be a satisfying nap and those words of his stung her worse than a scorpion from the jungle. Her ego was in overdrive. "Did he sense what I have been feeling all along?" she angrily blurted out to Annabelle, who was now rummaging around in the kitchen, completely unaware of Rachel's feelings. "Since his proclaimed awakening about three years ago, he does have some empathic abilities, so perhaps he knew that I needed to take my time" she continued, while the two of them got ready to walk to the nearest store and grab some easy food for dinner. "My insides hurt so badly" she said on the walk, as she doubled over in some sort of intestinal and emotional pain. She had felt all along that her and Jonathan's connection was strong, and they could literally feel what the other was feeling even from thousands of miles away, but she still wasn't convinced their connection was anything more than literary from the beginning. Annabelle rubbed her back while Rachel was bending forward in front of the grocery store, writhing in abdominal pain. It was as if her soul mate was also experiencing some sort of discomfort, despite the fact that he was the one who casually mentioned he had met someone else. She couldn't believe it. Annabelle wanted to buy her the best bottle of red wine and celebrate something. "But what is there to celebrate?" Rachel honestly and sadly questioned. "You have just been freed" Annabelle intimated in a very supportive and wise way. They were determined to sip some good wine with dinner, chat about wonderful moments in each other's lives, and forget about the words that he so eloquently wrote to her via email. She had wished he would have called to let her know this news, but he chose the easy route, which she knew all too well in her own past experiences. He explained his position in writing. "It's okay, I completely understand" were her thoughts after the shock had passed and she could stand up straight.

At first she was rather relieved. She felt that he needed to explore more on his own path prior to any reunion, if that was in fact, meant to happen. Then, she got angry; angry that she even considered this man to be a soul mate; angry that she chose to write her the "goodbye" instead of being a man and calling her. When Annabelle suggested they walk to the store, get a bottle of wine, and make dinner together to celebrate, initially Rachel was into it. Her doubling over in sincere gut pain was her body's way of processing his words. She couldn't recall a moment in her life where she actually got angry and wanted to hit some pillows. "Why am I so distraught over this? Is it because I was living in fantasy world and thinking I could live in Nicaragua and just hang by the beach all day, sort of like an escape?" she said to Annabelle as they walked home. The reality hit her that he had moved on. As she nibbled on the awesome perfect pairings of appetizers that Annabelle had assembled, she felt as if she had once again over-compromised her soul. Listening to Jonathan's story that entire late afternoon sitting on the beach sand well into the evening showed her more of a lesson. He was more ready for an intimate relationship with her than she was willing to give at that point, or at any time at all. The timing was off. And if that wasn't bad enough, a random phone call from William came through, and he told her he was moving back to Kansas in a month. He accepted a more lucrative job and needed to get unstuck. "Hmmm, that's interesting. "I thought divorcing his wife would have got him unstuck, but I guess the job situation was more important" she said to Annabelle who was admiring her cheese plate while they were sipping from a bottle of pinot. Rachel wasn't a drinker anymore. She chose to abstain from alcohol for a number of years and for several reasons, one of which was clarity in relationships. Every time she would have a glass or two of wine her inhibitions were completely tossed to the wayside, and her brain got foggy and stupid. Plus, it just messed with her sleep. During both her marriages she was used to imbibing a few glasses of wine almost every evening. It became habitual. Then she thought she might even have a problem with the addiction of wine. After her second divorce she sought counseling and her own style of "treatment" to investigate why she needed to drink wine every night. Her conclusion was that the alcohol made her forget just how emotionally disconnected she was in relationships. She then gave it up for years. The email from Jonathan gave her a reason to drink, or so she thought. She needed a cloudy messed up brain that night, so she and Annabelle each had two full glasses of the delicious liquefied grapes.

"After last night and a few too many glasses of wine, which was what I needed at the time, God, I think my few days with him were such a waste. Sounds like all he wanted was someone to satisfy his loneliness with a good ol' romp in the sack" she continued writing. "That's not me, God. I am so glad I chose to not go to Nicaragua to live. It would have been a disaster. I mean, where would I work and earn money? I couldn't have expected him to pay my bills and current debts, although he did promise I could write all day and be happy. Anyway God, I'm here in California, a place that always feels cozy and homey, and I'm going to continue on with seeing who I need to see and trusting the process of life. Thank you for listening. This is a short entry today because I am staying with Annabelle and she's being a most gracious host. Plus, we are off to run around the lake and look at the ducks. I love you, and thanks for sitting in my heart today." She noticed her penmanship getting sloppy and she wondered if it was the wine still talking. Either way, spilling her guts to her Higher Power gave her a deep sigh of relief.

She was sad. She was in the midst of a holiday trip and feeling blue. She was on a replenishment and restoration trip in California, and although the first part of the trip by the sunshine and beach was invigorating and expansive, the second part in Northern California gave her a big old gut ache. "How could I allow this man to affect me so deeply?" she surmised in every journal entry since the email from him. Her next step was to let it go. However difficult it was to hear his words that he met someone else, she needed to practice the awareness and detachment that she so vigorously worked on for years. "I think I'll miss the literary component more than ever" one of her journal entries stated. "I'm sure he's with some blonde bombshell" she continued in a very low self-esteem kind of way. "Time to restore my inner sanity and forward momentum, thank you" were the final sentences to God in a few post-Jonathan entries while in California.

After returning to her college city, where she began to feel a bit more connected and rooted, she had to immediately return to her vitamin job. A few vacation weeks without pay was enough to leave her bank account rather dry and have her wondering how she would be able to afford all of her fiscal responsibilities. If there was one thing William taught her, it was how to be more financially sound. She was never very good at maintaining a budget, yet now it was more important than ever, as she was preparing herself for greater things to come. She wasn't entirely sure what those greater things were, but she sure felt another wave of bigger moments happening in her life. With the past securely behind her, Jonathan declaring his love for someone else, she was ready to forge into new territory and submerge into securing her future. "I've never been one to save money, but now I feel as though I am about to go on some sort of traveling mission" she thought as she scurried around the kitchen performing her morning ritual of tea and chocolate. "This is probably the perfect time to join a book club and get involved with like-minded souls who want to explore the inner and outer workings of the mind" was her initial thought while pouring the first cup of tea. She was a unique soul. She was told that by many, but as she was somewhat reflective on what had transpired in the past few months, she felt as though she was being the most authentic she had ever been. It felt good. It felt right. She was fulfilling a purpose. She was on the road to her true destiny, despite her looking-for-love phase rearing its sordid head again in Nicaragua. As she was getting ready to punch a clock for the day job, she started to think about him. Deep inside, she had felt as though their friendship was not over. She was clearly aware of soul connections, and her relationship with him felt more like a kinship that she had never known. As patient as she was being, with both herself and the connection, she thought of their conversations and energy together and what was looming in her psyche. "Was Jonathan a soul mate?" "Did we meet at just the proper time in Nicaragua, only to go through the initial stages of this soul connection, and who knows what would happen next?" she continually asked the Universe. "I really need to talk this over with a group of women who delve into this stuff on a regular basis" she said attempting to widen her social circle. She was still in the midst of exploring this with him and completely willing to surrender to the Universe what it had planned for her. When she hooked up with a gregarious group of different-aged women, all brought together by her dear friend, Donna, she felt like she had some good ears and open hearts to dump her stuff. They never judged her. Every woman simply offered their words, each one listening to everyone's story. She met with these women once per month and they were her goddess group salvation. They would laugh over homemade pot luck meals, talk about recent books and movies, and celebrate their togetherness. She looked forward to the gatherings every month, and the next one couldn't come soon enough.

Meanwhile, she spent countless nights reading and studying the dynamics of a soul mate connection. It was sort of a continuation of her previous years, but it felt different this go-round. "People have lots of soul mates in their lives. They are teachers, mirrors, and karmic cleansers" she continued to write in her journal. She just had to let it go, continue to hold Jonathan in a compassionate light, remain forgiving, and be the friend that the two of them could ultimately become, if at all.

She knew that the only thing that mattered in this world was love. A complete transformation was happening right beneath her feet, she could feel it. She knew that there was a shift in the consciousness of society, and she was poised to be in the midst of a great love affair. She just wasn't sure how or when it was supposed to happen, or even who it was going to be with. Her road to fulfillment was left up to God. She had surrendered in past journeying phases, but this time her strength far surpassed previous free will occurrences. Destiny awaited her. "It's different now," she told her best girlfriend in Colorado. "I'm stronger, wiser, more patient, and refusing to repeat the past, as I don't feel my intuition even leads me in those situations" she continued to yell into her cell phone due to the surrounding traffic. "This was profound" she thought. Rachel and Jonathan were distant soul mates, and as much as she felt society was now in a position to reunite more of these types of relationships together, she continued to surrender every day and move forward with a purpose. She also took off the rose-colored glasses pertaining to him, and reality set in.

The Holiday Season

*D*ecember filled the air. The smells of autumn leaves gracefully floating on tree limbs, only to wistfully fall to the ground and dot each sidewalk in the neighborhoods with color and crunchy sounds. Leaf blowers were banned in her city, so she was able to take in all the significance of late autumn and the onset of early winter. It wasn't even that cold yet, but everyone seemed to wear sweaters and boots and scarves, despite the temperatures hovering in the 60's. The minute the clouds took over the blue sky and sun, more clothes donned people's bodies, and she found this amusing. "Don't these people even feel the weather, or are they programmed to wear what we are supposed to wear this time of year?" she smiled as she walked around the city accomplishing small errands on a Sunday in flip flops. She had the day off from the vitamin job, so her focus turned to creative pursuits. She put forth more effort into her storytelling and concocting healthy dishes to eat for the week. She felt Sundays were good for that type of activity, not to mention the wave of inspiration she felt after a solid hour of rigorous yoga and deep meditation prior to creating in the kitchen.

Seasons tended to come and go in her college city. The weather wasn't that big a factor in showing tons of color or snow, yet there was never any shortage of festive parties and celebrations that always involved way too much food and alcohol, and music piping from every venue around. Fortunately for Rachel, she was adverse to the temptation of drinking too much that made her feel like crap the next day. She also learned over the years that just saying "no" to too many treats and gastric blowouts was okay for her, and she never had to explain the reasons why she passed over several otherwise popular dishes. She had a way of smiling sweetly, gesturing gracefully, and moving about any social gathering with ease. It suited her just fine to not conform to what the other guests were always indulging in or talking about incessantly, which was probably gossip. She couldn't wrap her head around drama and gossip, as her family history of all that forced her into some serious soul-searching for many years. She felt she was now above the pettiness of it all.

The winter solstice was upon her ever-growing city, with nothing more than some cooler temperatures and blowing leaves in the wind. It was a subtropical climate and there was never a traditional changing of the seasons. She can't even remember the time it was brutally cold in her city. If anything the nights would be brisk and the days balmy. The only one noticeable setback to the lack of changing seasons in the college environs was the fact that every month brought up one allergy season after another. If it wasn't mold, it was grasses and weeds, as December notably had cedar fever on high alert. At first, she thought she was coming down with a terrible flu. At her vitamin job, where she was allowed to rummage through the free drawer of all the many homeopathic potions and drops and the numerous herbal remedies to combat allergic reactions, she couldn't get on top of the symptoms that were plaguing her on a daily basis. Her sleep was fragmented and she always had a stuffy nose and watery eyes. She was no fan of allergy season, and it occurred all year round. Days and months of the stagnant feeling had her dreaming of oceans and cliffs and tropical breezes and native flora, and no allergies. Her desire to move had come front and center again and because she was entering into a whole new phase of living, the question of where to go and how to get there was a topic of discussion in her subconscious. Living in the college city gave her those roots, but she had no resistance to settling elsewhere, as long as the new city, town, state, or country had its fair share of beauty, water, mountains, nature, and nice people.

"The holidays are a splendid time to enjoy family, friends, visits, good vibes, and just about anything that brings my people together" she confidently said to a nearby neighbor. She had an amazing opportunity to travel to Southern California prior to the scheduled holiday visit in Northern California, and she jumped at the chance. "I'm always open to traveling to the western ocean—always" she mentioned to her fellow passenger on the flight seated next to her, as she was secretly wishing the whole ordeal would be over soon. But she was excited to be spending ten full days by the beach, riding a beach cruiser left by her hosts of the condo where she was staying, and enjoying quiet time to reflect and replenish before the onslaught of family in Northern California. Traveling to California made her happy.

Every day in that Southern California condo was spent either doing long sessions of morning yoga, followed by a walk around the neighborhood that overlooked the ocean, capped off with a healthy breakfast of stir-fry veggies and eggs. It was a staple for her and it satisfied her tummy and made her feel comfortable. With her constant thoughts on food rationing, given her meager monthly paycheck, a colorful breakfast later in the day not only filled her up, but dinner was an afterthought with usually some fruit or a piece of cheese. "Ah, the simple life" she blurted out to the sky on an afternoon cruise by the sea. She was told how simple she was many times and the latest Thanksgiving trip was a testament to just how low maintenance she had become. Everything felt so incredibly perfect, even the Jonathan fiasco strengthened her in one way or another. She wasn't left to be a pile on the floor. She could pick herself up and move on. "Besides, he wasn't truly the man for me" said her subconscious on a morning run, as if to dismiss the importance of what transpired weeks before.

She straddled the beach cruiser bike every day, peddled up and down the coast, and felt extremely grateful that this was her only means of transportation for 10 days. "It's just like when I lived on the islands a few years ago" she whispered to the ocean as she cruised by. She didn't dare start up the luxury auto that sat in her friends' garage, knowing that it would be her full responsibility should something happen. Her southern California friends gave her the green light to use the new sporty car in case she needed it, but her gut told her to just keep riding the bike if there was somewhere she needed to go. She was able to meet up with an old friend for lunch, which turned out to be more of a classy place than her beach-cruising clothes prepared her for. Her attire was more of a cross between a yoga girl, a hippie chick, and a tropical beach gal. "Oh well, it's who I am" she mentioned casually to the girls sitting next to her on the bench outside in the waiting area. Turns out, both girls were heavily made up, legs crossed, looking uncomfortable, and commented that they wished they were on a bike riding in the California sunshine versus having to dress up for lunch. It was a reminiscing kind of afternoon and she left the classy lunch place knowing she probably would never return. There was something different about her relationship with the old friend. It wasn't her friend, per se, but Rachel herself. She was the different one. She was the one who felt as if all the work she had done over the years placed her in a category some might call "crazy". She had evolved and was continuing to shift and transform in ways that even baffled her. The remainder of her stay in the beach condo was so peaceful. She rode to her old favorite bookstore, hoping to reconnect with the two women who were so kind to her when she was going through all of her soul work. She used to walk into the store, small dog in tow, sit for hours reading one book excerpt after another—from astrology to tarot to mystics to anything that had anything to do with her purpose, which she had yet to realize. The two women always were compassionate and graceful and provided plenty of treats to Rachel's little dog at the time, who became like the store mascot. On that particular afternoon, both women weren't around when she dropped by to visit, so she left a note or two that she was in town for a few days and would love to see them again. She was forever grateful to them. She then hopped back on the beach cruiser bike and peddled further up the coast to the meditation gardens overlooking the vast sea. It was her spiritual bliss for one or two afternoons each week, way back in the good old lively Southern California days. It brought back one memory after another, all cozy and fuzzy feeling. She locked up the bike and entered into the gardens to sit amongst the most beautiful flora ever. She stayed for a good solid hour or so, sitting on a concrete ornate bench that graced many of the intricate gardens. It was her favorite. Something about the position of the bench, facing the ocean, being able to watch surfers and dolphins and sunsets and possibly sunrises (although she was never up early enough for the latter), made her feel as though the current trip back to the special area, returning to see her old friends, and cruising the same parts she used to call home, gave her a final sense of completion. Her meditation was all about gratitude.

She left the gardens that afternoon, peddled back down the coast to the condo, and settled in for the evening. She wrote about her gratitude in her journal. If she wasn't riding the bike up and down the coast, she was running somewhere near the ocean, or walking the pretty neighborhood, or watching a movie on the technologically complicated T.V., or taking a nap. The T.V. alone was a bit of a challenge, and since she didn't own a television, she was intrigued by the three remote controls, the surround sound, the hundred million channel options, and a question of "does anyone really watch all these channels?" With the T.V. programmed to the soundscape station playing one peaceful song after another, she was able to write and write some more. It was what she was meant to do, more than anything on the trip. She spent many an afternoon writing to her heart's content. No distractions, no loud traffic noises, no phone calls, no nothing; just her pen and paper.

The remainder of her holiday visit to Southern California had a few slight guilt trips associated with it. Self-imposed, no doubt, but she wanted to be sure she owned all of her stuff in her new life. First of all, she had stopped drinking wine years ago after her second divorce. She felt as though she needed the clarity of thinking to further her into more deep soul work. Alcohol only clouded her mind, made her do stupid things like texting the wrong person at the wrong time, and possibly saying something she would never say sober. It wasn't as if she drank a lot in the good old days, she simply liked to get a buzz. With the exception of the Jonathan bust-up and needing wine at that moment, she had abstained for three solid years to pursue her souls' journey. However, she decided to indulge in a glass or two on the southern California trip. "California is practically made up of vineyards and grapes, so I might as well blend in with the landscape" she rationalized to herself. It seemed rather silly and perfect, all the same. The vibe was right, the ambiance was calling her name, and she was in the mood. Granted, she was alone, so the thought of some sort of alcoholism went running through her brain, but she always felt she never had a problem. It was her husband and lovers who had the problem, and she was simply an enabler. Now single, she felt like a nice glass of wine to go with her expensive French cheese and a feeling of relaxation. "The first sip tastes so incredibly good and I have zero guilt about it because I know that balance is important at this stage of my life" was her subconscious going into overdrive. One glass later she was done, and continued on with her writing, walking, meditation, and just a general feeling that everything was going to be okay. She thought about another glass, but recalled one too many texts to past lovers where she wished she would have just kept her mouth shut. It was yet another mantra for her new life. Just as she boarded the plane to carry on with her holiday travels to Northern California, she knew her brother was a collector of old vintage bottles, and her entire family was going to be gathering for their annual turkey day festivities. Only this time the family dynamic was different. Her oldest brother had split from his long-term marriage, their only ethereal daughter was soon to be a teenager, and both parties from the marriage were now in other relationship patterns. At times it seemed complicated, other times just a nuisance. She landed in Northern California, was picked up at the airport by Annabelle's sister who lived nearby, and deposited at her townhome in the charming town by the bay. It wasn't exactly the oceanfront property but close enough to smell it. Staying at the townhome with all the kids nearby, who happened to be cousins of Rachel's niece was dizzying enough, trying to figure out who belonged to whom. It was Thanksgiving and chaos amongst family members was a given. She was always dubbed "the glue" of the family. "Now I feel I'm like the peaceful warrior; the daughter who is a published author; the sister who had some serious boundaries when it came to love and relationships; and the friend who is willing to listen and understand anything that comes up within a conversation over a smooth glass of wine" was her offering up her own explanation of who she was in her mind. It was one of the best Thanksgivings that she could remember in years gone by. The family members were much older, more mature, more evolved themselves, and extremely helpful in giving insight to problems that seemed so small, but were actually larger than life. Rachel and her older brother managed to sneak away one afternoon from all the hoopla and go for a long bike ride through the trail system that runs throughout the town. The paths were lined with oak trees turned all sorts of oranges and reds and yellows, ducks emerging from the nearby lake, kids roller skating with Mom's jogging next to them, runners of all shapes and sizes, and every breed of dog imaginable. It was a bonding experience for them; one they hadn't taken in over ten years or so. Her brother needed some advice on the new girlfriend and the merging of families. Rachel had no experience of this, per se, but was willing to listen and offer some words of wisdom from past experiences of friends. "Give it about three years before the kids warm up to you. Keep being there for them, showing love and support, and they will eventually understand your place in their world" was all she could offer her brother during a snack break of sweet potato fries on an amazingly gorgeous afternoon. The weather was crisp, clear, sunny, and perfect. Together, they seemed to have a mutual understanding of what needed to happen during that bike ride. While perched on a concrete ledge bordering the town's park they had the conversation about the new families and where it's all going. She loved every minute of it because it showed her that her brother trusted her words and nothing more needed to be said. They ate their fries, which tasted awesome after sweating for a few miles on the bike, and they sat in silence for much of the noshing, each licking the salt from their fingertips. Afterwards, they mounted back onto their cycles, ran a few errands, pretended to lock up the bikes during a walkabout the town, and rode back home. The charming rich town never had a crime issue, and it was displayed in their ability to just lean their bikes up against a post and leave them alone for an hour or two. She thought this could never happen in her college city back home. "Those bikes would have been gone within minutes" she thought.

The ride back to the house was just as harmonious and invigorating, only the temperature began to drop and she wasn't prepared for the chill. She didn't care. She was having breakthroughs with a family member. But once home they reconvened with the other siblings and aunts, watched some football, cooked in mass quantities, talked only about random subjects, and enjoyed the remainder of the Thanksgiving affair. It was full of every dish for the creative cuisine expert, sans turkey. Although the turkey was the common main dish for every one of her family holidays, it wasn't meant to be on that day. The turkey took longer than normal and the family completely forgot about it as they had so many other tasty and filling side dishes to eat. Once the turkey was finished it was well past dessert time, and the big bird was saved for leftovers the following days and weeks to come. No one even complained that the main part of the feast was missing.

After the week of being with family was over, Rachel felt she had endured many new beginnings and poignant endings as well. The email from Jonathan was an ending, and she was grateful. The newfound energy with her brother and his intermingled family was enchanting and happy, so that was a beginning. The phone call from William from months gone by, saying he was moving and accepting a lucrative position in another state was an ending, yet it was also a beginning of sorts. The interesting and confusing relationship never ever felt done to either of them. There were new definitions, new boundaries. Something felt like it ended for her, but a beginning was looming in her midst. "Was it related to

William?" she thought on her final hike through the redwood forest adjacent to her brother's house. For the first time in a long time, she had big swoops of contentment take over her heart. It wasn't always pretty, and oftentimes painful, but she managed to respond to actions versus overreact. It was a great step towards her purpose.

As she said her goodbyes to her brother and niece the following day, the sighs of relief that the holidays were over gave her pause. It was only Thanksgiving after all, and a day and time that was most important to her mother more than anything. With Christmas on the horizon she knew she could once again be introspective and quiet, as needed. The Christmas holiday was more about getting together with a few orphan friends who chose to remain in the city rather than be with family, and not travel during the chaotic weather and crowd mess that tends to plague all the airports. Christmas was peaceful and full of even more thoughts of new beginnings. As she boarded the plane home following a congenial goodbye to her brother, the girlfriend, his daughter, Annabelle, her boyfriend, and her sister, it was clear that the Thanksgiving holiday trip was meaningful in so many ways. It was needed and necessary and it furthered her perspective on the meaning of "new beginnings." Another new moon eclipse was happening in December, followed by an end-of-year full moon; it gave her the impetus to continue to move forward, ban all negativity from past, present, and future. "I am into that stuff" she said to the slow-moving stewardess who asked her to push her stuff further under the seat. It was then that she glanced down at the wide amethyst bracelet on her wrist and was ready to usher in the changes.

The Violet Flame

No amount of research and spiritual understanding could prepare her for a deep personal transformation. She wanted to believe all things happened for a reason, yet it required intention, work, awareness, understanding, and being fully awake for the process. It also took exorbitant amounts of patience. Strength and courage were all part of the process for her. "I have boundaries now, I no longer align myself with negativity, I know how to say no, and no one can bend my will for me" she said imagining herself throwing a hat up into the sky while twirling around like Mary Tyler Moore. She certainly had her fair share of mistakes and imperfections, but this time around she was so incredibly strong and realistically able to move forward. She felt out of the thick draggy muck. While she meandered through the streets and neighborhood of her ever-growing city, a city that used to be even smaller before all the technology and overgrowth of urban sprawl took over, she felt gratitude once again. It was at that moment she again gazed down at her wrist and the big fat amethyst bracelet that was given to her on her birthday months ago, and she pondered the meaning of it all. "Why am I always needing a thing to catapult me into a different sphere?" she said foolishly to her only plant in her small sublet. She researched amethyst crystals and what owning a piece of this gem meant in the big picture. She was rather unfamiliar with crystals and the overall message, as her old self was always into the jewels that made her feel luxurious. But not now. Wearing an amethyst bracelet was healing, warded off negative energy, and helped with alcoholism. "Hmmm, hope it wasn't given to me because Donna thought I had a problem!" she nervously mentioned to the same plant that listened to most of her stories. What she found awesome and perfect was that amethyst crystals aided in spiritual practices and transformational journeys. "Ah, this is what it's all about for me" her newly confident self said while looking up at the sky and taking the trash out to the nearby bin. "My soul is prepared for this transformation, and I can thank Donna each and every time I look at the bracelet" she once again mused to the lonely plant.

What stood out in her ping pong mind at that moment was that she recently remembered her Dad had gone to a prestigious school in Ohio named Kenyon College. It was a small liberal arts school that produced some mighty fine authors and artists. "Hmmm" she thought on a run one day. "Maybe it's in my DNA to be a writer and author" was her major thought as she bundled up in the unusually chillier weather that predominated her college city. Although the city was located in a subtropical zone she still had to endure the winters of colder and drier temperatures, yet it was nothing compared to the brutal summers of consistent days of high heat and humidity. "I can't complain at all" she once told a neighbor while they were getting their mail. She actually felt strong in the cold knowing her hot bath following an intense exercise session outside was just around the corner.

The violet flame had captured her attention on more than one occasion. It wasn't an actual flame, per se, but the meaning behind the notion of what the violet flame represented and how it can manifest into a transmutation of negative vibrations into one godly spiritual connection like never before certainly peaked her curiosity. It was similar to a Phoenix rising, and one which she felt like she was going through every time she stepped outside into the public eye. Even her vitamin job was losing its steam and she just wanted to spend her days writing, doing yoga, running, meet up with socially responsible people, travel a bit, and live an incredibly good life of love and happiness with no drama, similar to the sabbatical island living. She was done with drama, that's for sure. The violet flame notion kept popping into her subconscious and she researched it on the internet as often as she had the time.

The precipice of a new year beckoned with her feeling so incredibly different. It was as if this newfound surrender of hers kept her balanced and solid. She slept with the amethyst bracelet under her perfect pillow every night. She wore the bracelet every day, even switching from right to left wrist every so often, simply because it was different. She was almost making herself ill with all the violet flame connotations that she tried to manifest. "Am I overdoing it, Universe?" she asked while waiving her amethyst-adorned hand into the sky. Every time she entered the doors to the vitamin job she would hold her wrist in the air to ward off negative vibes from needy and difficult people. Her research about crystals and their power left her feeling like she was a bit of a step ahead of the life game, at least in her mind. She had a colorful and active brain, one in which coworkers would roll their eyes at on occasion, not to mention William. Her practical and reality side was somewhat nonexistent during these years, but she kept at it. When her friend gave her the bracelet Rachel wasn't much of a big jewelry girl, but the fat purple bracelet looked cool and unique and it was certainly a facet of life that she was now embracing. While stretching out her mat in the living room to do her own version of home yoga, she placed the bracelet to grace the side of the mat for extra good measure. It was almost too cumbersome to wear during rigorous yoga shoulder poses, as the crystals would stick into her skin and almost cause severe pock marks. The amethyst bracelet became the center of her world, and it definitely had some meaning. It was a synchronistic sign to much going on in her life and she knew about synchronicity from her past days of soul-searching, even before living in Bali. The violet flame was alive and well, as represented by the big fat deep purple crystal bracelet that was a fixture on her wrist.

Life was continuing on into the New Year and the vitamin job was still thumping along, with a few extra responsibilities thrown in much to her dismay. She wanted to keep the job part time, simple, and fun, but the powers-that-be had chosen to dump a few new technical aspects to the job, which certainly required more hours. She found it all a bit overwhelming. She wasn't much of a technical person either as this made her brain go cuckoo, but she obliged, watched the video on how to perform certain new tasks, and emerged from the viewing room as if she was hit by a large bus. It wasn't a pretty sight and her coworkers asked "are you okay?" which Rachel replied "I just need a few minutes (she was thinking more hours in her creative brain) to process what I just watched and I'll get back to you". It was early in the day for all this technical viewing to be taking place. It made her tired and feeling like the vitamin job wasn't as fun as it used to be. She was bored and overwhelmed. It was then that she reverted to what made her happy and feeling alive. She started dancing and acting like the old aerobics queen she used to be back in the early 1980s. Her coworkers laughed and got on board and the entire wellness department was transformed into a very upbeat environment, grape vining from one aisle to the next. She just had that kind of impact on people, and she began to realize that her actions and words were more than just offbeat and unusual. She could totally affect the mood which gave her reassurance that her purpose was validated. Wearing the amethyst bracelet to work every day helped to set the tone for change in a stressful wellness environment, or so she thought. The vitamin store was the busiest one in town and taking a thirty-minute reprieve each day to see the sun break through the clouds each day brought more happiness to her than she knew what to do with. Just warding off the negative vibe that tended to permeate the store on a daily basis was part of her subconscious plan. People always came in sick and needy and she did her best to help, but on some days it was simply too much. "Having the amethyst bracelet around my wrist transmutes all negative energy into love, abundance, prosperity, happiness, and peace," she whispered to her favorite younger co-worker. It was her purpose. The violet flame was rising more and more within her and she felt better than ever. Even her dreams and sleep were more profound and peaceful. She chalked this up to placing the bracelet under her pillow at night, and it became a ritual. Her hot flashes waned a bit, her dream images were extremely vivid, and she woke up rested and ready to move into her home yoga program. If she wasn't doing yoga to classical music at home, she was lacing up her running shoes and exploring her little neighborhood. "I can see and run through this place for the umpteenth time, hear a new bird chirping, pet a new dog on my path, or rummage through a song in my head to keep me going, that is what life is about" was her personal testament. She was on a grand path. Even William had tried to re-enter in the same old fashion, but she had placed boundaries on her heart's involvement with him. His business was still unfinished and she chose to be a bit selfish on how she spent her time. After years of giving away her energy to those who weren't grateful or in need, she decided now to focus her positive and soulful energy on her purpose and it was unfolding every single day. The amethyst bracelet, coupled with the violet flame integration, had given her reasons to feel profoundly happy. "Life is truly something to behold," she wrote as a post on her social networking site hoping for many clicks and views and thumbs ups.

She woke up the next morning, excited to go for a run and somewhere different than her own neighborhood. It took her hours to get going, as she didn't have to punch the clock in the morning, nor did she have any pressing commitments, other than a few phone calls, articles to write for various publications, and meeting the dog owner who she was planning to house sit for in the coming days. After many cups of hot green tea on the chilly, foggy, misty morning, she laced up her shoes, loaded up into the rolling olive and drove to the water, with the amethyst bracelet in tow.

The lake in the middle of the city had many trail variations that she could choose from; one was four miles, five miles, seven miles, and the bigger loop of ten miles. She decided she was going to punch out a five-miler on that ominous morning. Something about no one being at the lake, which was extremely popular most every day and the hub for the see and be seen, it was her feelings that running in the rain was romantic which led her to the water. "Reminds me of a Hemingway novel," she blurted out randomly to the interior of the Fiat as she found a convenient place to park. The prevalent sea of bright running wear worn by the local people who were desperately trying to stick to their New Year's resolutions, was virtually gone. She had the lake all to her lonesome and loved it. As she trotted on the trail with a relatively brisk pace noticing the swans peacefully gliding on the water, the egrets sitting calmly on the large pieces of wood jutting out of the lake, and the water being an exceptionally green-blue color, a very tall attractive man was running in her direction. He didn't have much clothing on at all on the chilly morning, but he looked good. Lithe, muscular, older, good solid running gait, the gentleman came within about five feet of her space and uttered the words "pick it up, sister!" She was shocked. For one thing she had no idea the man would say anything other than a simple "hi", which is common amongst runners crossing each other on the lake, or a kind gesture of a head nod. The relatively hot guy decided to blurt out the words that she so fondly remembered in her own coaching days, way back when. She used to coach adults and high school runners on everything from running economy to what shoes to buy and what to look for when buying those shoes, to where to run, to how fast to train, and always what to eat.

They were her best young days of her life. She loved being a running coach. Apparently when the tall and handsome dude decided to coach her in a quick one-sentence way, she did what anyone would do who is on the receiving end of a good coach, she picked up her pace. Fortunately, she was at the end of the trail and her five-mile wet soggy run, but that didn't deter her from being appreciative of that man on her path and his rather bold statement to her. She was willing to listen. After all, she did have an amethyst bracelet in her possession. She wasn't fond of too many clunky things while running, especially too much clothing, but she had to keep the bracelet on for posterity. If anything she was better off with less clothing, as her hot flashes would always flare up at the most inopportune times and she would end up shedding a layer or two.

"Was this the violet flame appearing as a tall runner man?" her flighty subconscious reminded her while she stretched on the bridge. The bridge that spanned across part of the pond was the perfect place for her to extend her leg onto the railing and continue with her limber ways.

She scooted into the Fiat seat, sweaty hamstrings and all, found an old coconut water drink in the glove box and drank it to her heart's delight. "I wonder if this is still good or will it give me some sort of stomach ache?" she mused while turning the radio up banging her head side to side with Nine Inch Nails. She shifted gears and turned the corner to head back to her sublet on the northwest side, complete with the spiritual sweat-laced amethyst bracelet gracing her wrist.

Contentment

Waking up from dreams night after night was always either disturbing to her in some way, shape, or form; or she felt completely motivated and inspired by the images she remembered from her dreams. Oftentimes she felt as though her dreams were a prelude to what was coming or what had already happened, or what she was repressing. She made it a habit to examine her dreams upon waking up, reading the definition of each image either online or in her dream dictionary book. She pretty much left no stone unturned when it came to growth and movement within her own being. Rachel always loved to explore the deep inner workings of her soul, and her dreams were yet another reason she felt compelled to progress on her path. "I am one crazy chick, that's for sure" she would tell her emotionally reluctant mother whenever she had the chance.

Hence the phone call that came that chilly and rainy morning. She was on another dog-sitting gig in a nearby neighborhood, as she relished in every time her name was chosen by potential people needing a good human companion to stay with their dogs or cats every time they left town. She put her name on a reputable website and so far had received four solid appointments to watch and protect the many animals in her care. She also loves it, for it gave her a reason to stay in someone else's home, explore a new neighborhood, and make her feel like she's on a mini-vacation. As she was enjoying the simple luxuries of a flat screen T.V. and other amenities that she no longer had, the phone rang, and it was William. "How ironic as I have been thinking about you for the past few weeks?" She mentioned to him as he was about to ask a very though-provoking question. Since he had moved away months ago she was certain that her newfound freedom would do her some good. But, she couldn't stop thinking about him. He sounded so wonderful on the phone to her. His voice was soothing, his words were flowing, and she missed him terribly. They chatted about easy stuff and catching up on the latest news about each other's coming and goings, from writing projects to his new consulting work to their respective city's happenings, and finally, to his question. "I was wondering if you would be interested in coming on a vacation to Mexico with me?" was how he nervously worded his inquiry. She couldn't quite believe what she was hearing, as she had mentioned the fact they had never traveled together in their two years of being involved. For some strange reason she always felt traveling together was a good indication of how couples can cohabitate in living situations. He wasn't big on vacations due to the expense, so that alone was an odd thing for him to say. "Well, what were you thinking and when?" she asked in return. He wanted to go to Puerto Vallarta, as he had amassed thousands of hotel points, which would pay for a 10-day getaway at a resort on a beach. "Oh my goodness!" she exuberantly exclaimed. "I am shocked, nervous, excited, confused, and completely ready to go on a vacation to the beach". Although she had spent about a month in California over the holidays, it wasn't the same. The beaches in California were a hit and miss when it came to ocean temperature. She wasn't fond of floating around in the blue sea in a wetsuit due to the waters only reaching a high of sixty degrees. "But the Caribbean, the waters can be a toasty 75 degrees or so" she intimated to him, and he agreed. He wasn't putting any pressure on her whatsoever, and that also felt good. He simply wanted to reinvigorate their relationship in a way that made sense to both of them; the beach. They both loved the ocean, talked about living by the ocean, dreamed of traveling to the ocean, and then his proposal-a possible ocean quest. She accepted his offer and from a distance they began to plan what was the beginning of a new solid life that she so desperately wanted years ago when they first met. The vacation was merely a step to some big changes that William was going through. He had shifted, and she was sure the Universe was working overtime on their behalf. When they first met and were heavily involved, he wasn't ready at that time to make any drastic moves on getting a divorce and committing to another long-term relationship. She was also away on her island sabbatical and pursuing a relationship would compromise her reasoning for being away. "Understandably so" thought Rachel, as she was more than ready. "But, was I really?" she began to ask herself after she hung up the phone and thought back to how their relationship evolved. They both seemed to be on the same page. He even mentioned the idea of moving back to the college city where she was currently living and where their romance was initiated. "Am I ready for that too?" she continued to ask herself while driving to the vitamin job. Her only questions came in silence. On one particular day while taking a lunch break outside during a clock-punching day a teeny ladybug flew onto her forehead. It actually landed on her third eye. Instead of swatting it away not knowing what the bug was, she let it do its thing. She instantly felt calm and composed and knew this was a sign of something. It migrated to her shoulder then her legs, and finally launched into the air and somewhere peaceful, which she didn't truly bother to look. She just knew the ladybug was safe.

When she returned to the job after that awesome and simple ladybug sign, she looked it up on the internet, the meaning of the calm and colorful little bug. "If a ladybug lands on your third eye it is a sign of higher intuition and trust. Since ladybugs have not a care in the world, they are showing you that life is okay." It was the definition of the meaning that she had read on the internet and after mentioning the ladybug synchronicity to a few trusted co-workers, she remembered what came up for her in morning meditation. "Let go and let God" were the words she uttered in surrender. Because of all the recent developments with William, she was beginning to think that the violet flame and its significance had taken hold of her. She had banished the past. Her karma was cleansed. She was living in the present. She was going to Puerto Vallarta with a man she had truly loved for years. She was content. "I feel he is no longer a complicated mess" she playfully whispered in the ear of the dog that was in her care for a few days. She read a poignant quote somewhere "Contentment had no rules. Contentment had no fear. Contentment was all about love." "Where did I read that?" her subconscious calmly asked. It didn't matter.

She was about to share her life with William, the man who had been a complicated mess for many years, yet was now on a path that resonated with her. As astounding as the cycle of life was for her she always believed in new moons, full moons and their meanings. If anything, she needed to share her life with a man. She needed to be in an emotionally intimate and romantic relationship again after almost seven years without. She needed to know that, after the age of fifty, life can be extremely content. Since she was still scratching her head on the notion of them as partners, she knew deep in her gut that he was the man who truly never left her side. He was always there, despite his marriage. He just didn't know how to end a nine-year union in a logical, respectful manner. He had never done it before, so he wanted to make sure it was amicable. "I totally get it" she said to him one day, as she offered her own experiences of leaving marriages that no longer worked, but never wanted the ending to get ugly. "Walking away with your dignity intact is surely a sign that you are more than ready for the next chapter" she also surmised, while feeling extremely wise in consulting his situation. Whenever they spoke they were more than on the same page. Gone were the dilemmas, the roller coaster rides, the insecurities, the questions, the jealousies. Their newfound partnership was all about contentment. "Just in time too, as I'm entering menopause and that's a whole new ball of wax in a relationship!" she excitedly mentioned to her close friend in California.

But first they had to get through 10 days in Mexico together. One step at a time, as already the plan had changed twice with great amounts of yelling and discomfort. That old familiar feeling of over-compromising crept up in her psyche.

She still felt as though a trip together could reveal more than she would know by staying in the same place. "If you don't change the scenery, the scenery never changes" was another one of her catchy inspirational sayings her subconscious told her on a sunny day. The itinerary was all set. Except they changed courses and were going to Cancun. Too many complications and third party flakiness created a whirlwind of emotions between them. They shouted obscenities at each other. They hung up on each other. They were projecting one feeling after another on each other. It was like a big storm before any calm. She had such a headache from all the drama. He was an over-thinker, and his reacting to words and their energy connection created a pounding in her head that made her want to reach for a wine bottle. But, she chose some old carrot juice from the refrigerator, took a massive amount of deep breaths, was grateful he was still out of town and out of reach, and she couldn't wait to spend the evening with some trusted girlfriends as planned. Something about the woman connection when he was spinning out of control gave her peace. She still wasn't 100 percent sure that the relationship was going to take off again. It was such a work in progress for her. If anything, with all the altered plans of late, she reflected on her own spontaneous behavior and decided that he was uncomfortable with all of the changes and was projecting that energy onto her. Either way, it wasn't simple in her book. So she went out, bought a new pair of super comfortable somewhat ugly supportive shoes for the vitamin job and went home and lay in the sun by the pool. That's what felt best at that moment and she went with it, having minimal clothing and feeling free.

The Beginning
is the End

"I can't believe he has changed the plan from Puerto Vallarta to Cancun, AGAIN!" she exclaimed in an email to her newfound soul sister, Annabelle. The two of them had grown so much closer, as Annabelle was finding her way out of the marriage to Rachel's brother and entering into her own spiritual realm of higher good and service. "Like attracts like" she said to her one day when Annabelle wasn't sure about their friendship. She began dating a younger massage entrepreneur, and Rachel felt that she could relate to the younger man syndrome. Annabelle became an important confidante in her new world. The two were able to discuss absolutely everything from sex to hormones, difficult situations in life, the dilemma of making plans, the astrological differences between a Taurus and a Libra and what to possibly expect (as they both knew a little something about each sign), spiritual practices, life changes, traveling, and everything in between. Gratitude was shown from both Annabelle and Rachel each time they spoke on the phone or had a dream about the other and their direction in life, or sent lengthy emails detailing graphic stuff about their respective new boyfriends and sex lives. It was the only release she had in a long while. No other girlfriend was able to share that kind of information, and she couldn't be happier about it. Every emotion that she felt was somehow translated in a way that Annabelle understood. They just seemed to get each other at a poignant stage of their lives.

After a rather tumultuous weekend with William wrought with confusion and expectations, she emailed Annabelle to give her the lowdown. She needed some sort of validation that the conversation intensity between her and William was a good thing. They spent the entire previous Saturday evening uncovering some incredible truths. He was stubborn. He wasn't going to back down on his point regarding how she had a tendency to not divulge everything about everything. She was vague at times simply answering his questions with little detail, and over the years they had known each other this wasn't going to fly with him anymore. Through his own maturity and transformation he needed more and his integrity felt at stake. He interrogated Rachel about her time in the jungle back in the mid-summer. His questions exhausted her. "So what exactly happened there and did you sleep with that dude?" was his abrupt way of phrasing his latest interrogation. "Let me sit you down and look you in the eye and not blink and tell you exactly what happened" was Rachel doing her best to appease the situation, all the while knowing that he didn't believe a word she was offering about the jungle trip. That was a very sensitive time for Rachel as her and William were on the outs due to his own complicated messy situation, and she felt that it was sort of sacred in a way. Her affording to go to another country, staying in minimal conditions, and having a random meeting with an interesting literary companion was just way too personal for her. He pressed on "you aren't being truthful with me regarding what transpired in Nicaragua" he kept insisting. The more stubborn he was on this point the louder her voice became. "I AM TELLING YOU THE TRUTH!" she literally screamed to him while he was fiddling around in the laundry room. "I want to trust you, but your free spirited ways are just too much for me, and I have my values and right now my integrity is at stake!" he raised his voice to her from the laundry room. She knew in the depth of her soul that she was being honest about not sleeping with Jonathan during her ten days in Nicaragua. "Once I say what I mean I don't need to explain any further" she mumbled under her breath, after being about as stern as she had ever been with him. "You DO need to explain further because I don't believe a damn word you are saying" he blurted back. "I am getting out of here! You are exhausting, and I don't even know why we are together at all" she confidently said to him while repacking her overnight bag she routinely took to stay over at his house. She was a new woman and those days of looking for love were long gone. "You'll never be convinced and I'm tired of being around you right now" she slammed the door behind her and he didn't go after her. "I don't need to end up in bed with any new potential lover, like before" she continued on while loading her stuff in the car. He was not listening to her anymore, so she might as well have been talking to the sky. Jonathan and Rachel were merely literary friends, and after all the drama and hubbub over the holidays where he was concerned, she wasn't going back. She felt nothing more for the smooth talker whatsoever, and ironically was feeling more for William than ever before, yet this latest mistrusting argument was about all she could take not to throw an iron at him or something. When she got frustrated, her usual tendency to respond gently went out the window. This time she reacted with harsh but truthful words. "Even Jonathan's mind seems rather insignificant, which I know was the basis for our random meeting." "Perhaps my interaction with him a few months ago was supposed to teach me more about relationships" she felt on many days, and especially now that he was in her face regarding the truth. "I've always felt that when you tell the truth there is no need to continue to convince why" she again repeated to her brain while gazing out the window one morning and listening to the birds sing. He was about the most stubborn man she had ever known, and had some jealousy issues to work out. He also had more moral fibers than any man she had ever been involved with on an intimate level, and was convinced that she had slept with Jonathan in the jungle. "That's your stuff!" she barked back at him on another afternoon when he wouldn't let it go. "I admit that I don't back down during a quality fight!" he surmised when they went at it again during her creative time of chopping vegetables and experimenting with spices for dinner. "Honestly?" "I can't do this again. I've got nothing left on this matter, and you better damn well let it go, or I am so gone for good" she said thinking her vegetable paring knife to his throat might back him down. "You are zapping all my creative energy with your constant questions and drama" her voice began to rise a bit. "I can't let it go right now!" "It's not that easy for me" he shouted from the bedroom, while she was stewing and wondering why her domestic skills were being compromised at that moment. She bit her lip and kept her mouth shut, and there was silence for a moment. He walked out of the bedroom and told her to leave. Without hesitation and olive oil splattering all over the stove from the preheated pan, she walked to the bedroom, grabbed her perfect pillow and backpack and headed for the door. She always took the pillow with her to his house. It reminded of her old drool pillow as a child, and with the tension between her and him, she needed a security backup to hold onto. It also helped correct imbalances in her neck, it cost an arm and a leg, and made her feel safe.

She was so tired of fighting with him on this whole point of honesty. It was not how she envisioned their newfound relationship beginning. They were in a revolutionary stage, or "probationary" stage, as she called it. They were testing the waters again. Even though it had only been a few months since he had returned from Kansas, he found his confidence again. "Is he my teacher in one way or another?" she mentioned to Annabelle, who was always there to listen to her heartfelt questions. "I swear, this is such a roller coaster ride and I'm about to get off for good!" she frustratingly said to Annabelle during the latest phone call. "Thanks for listening and responding to my call right away, as I so needed to be talked off the ledge" she continued while winding up the conversation where she ranted left and right to Annabelle for longer than necessary. "Just hang in there, this is more levels to the process" Annabelle replied. "You're now unpeeling more of the onion." Annabelle felt that her new beginning was interesting and certainly something to be nervous about. She herself had experienced similar interactions with her young massage lover, yet they were three years into a most blissful relationship. But still, "I'm a little wary" Annabelle wrote to her in a text, despite them hanging up the phone a few minutes earlier. "I get it. I'll sit with this recent dilemma for a while before I contact him again." And with those words, she sat in lotus position to re-center herself and breathe about as deeply as she could.

Over the years what she had learned and was now putting into practice was how to seriously relate on an emotionally intimate level. The dynamic with him wasn't just some test anymore. It was the real deal. He may just as well be her teacher on many levels. Annabelle also validated that point, and both Rachel and Annabelle were feeling as though the Mexico trip would be the most revealing stage of her transformation within the relationship with him. Every conversation with Annabelle during the phase of the new beginning with him revealed more and more. If anything, she knew and felt that any more communications with Jonathan were final and over. She knew that whatever she felt for him at that time after the vacation in the jungle was simply another step into becoming a more whole human being, which readied her to be truly intimate with William in a revolutionizing kind of way. Her "complicated-mess-of-a-boyfriend" no longer seemed complicated. It was introducing the whole Jonathan connection into the mess that showed her the intricacies of her emotional depths with William. Annabelle drove the point home, as she had similarly experienced the sameness with her young lover. She was in a new beginning with him to possibly learn that the end of any other past karmic connections were now over and done with at last. The new beginning was the end of the past. She was more than thankful to Annabelle, and they both solidified their soul sisterhood with tears, gratitude, and immense amounts of bonding in spirit. "Just give him what he needs and he will be yours forever" were her final words on another one of their many post-drama phone calls. "Does this imply that I have to put out more than usual?" She reluctantly inquired to Annabelle, who had a much stronger libido than Rachel. Annabelle had already hung up and she was left to ponder exactly what she meant.

Prelude to Mexico

Already the intensity between them was more than noticeable, even right down to the way they packed for vacations. She was more of a living-in-the-moment kind of gal. He was a planner, a strategist, and so very practical that it often made her wonder what the heck she was doing with someone completely her opposite. As the trip approached she had made sure she went through the motions of asking for the time off at her vitamin job, doing the diligence to make sure that when she returned she still had some sort of income to fall back on. Although the vitamin job wasn't her passion or career she didn't quite have the income as a full-time writer yet to support her daily living, which was extremely meager at best. All she truly needed was a massage every now and again, her pedicures, a decent haircut, groceries, and an occasional new pair of comfy shoes. "I have simplified my life to the point where I live within my means and I don't really need much, other than the self-care that makes me so happy and peaceful" she always surmised to her coworkers at the vitamin job, who wondered how she managed to live so well on so little. She almost felt a bit guilty that she afforded herself tiny luxuries, "but what the hell, I deserve it, right?" she continually said to God when she made a pedicure appointment. She had everything she wanted and needed at that time.

He was a bit anxious about the trip to Mexico. He hasn't vacationed since he got sober three years ago, and any trip to a resort could possibly tempt him to party and drink. But he was older and wiser now and felt going with her would be relaxing at best. She knew how to relax, that's for sure. Their differences were pretty obvious to both of them, but they now embraced and accepted that fact, yet still managed to roll their eyes at each other regarding some habitual nuances that each one possessed. It was all part of their new beginning.

As they sat by the pool at his apartment complex gazing up at the ever-changing clouds in the pretty royal blue sky talking about the trip, she felt a deep and profound love for him. It was a love that never truly went away. It was a love that kept coming back around, taking on different shapes and flavors and inspiring her on every level. He was a grounded and logical man. "How can him being such a stick in the mud inspire me?" she wondered quite a bit on every run she took in her cozy neighborhood. After several well-timed minutes by William relaxing near the pool looking up at the sky they walked back to his place continuing to talk about so much more than just surface topics. He then looked down, picked up a penny, mentioned to her about the nickel he found on the road hours earlier, and proceeded to unlock the door to his apartment. She stood there for a moment digesting what he said and did regarding the coins, smiled from ear to ear, and proceeded to go in. "It's really my thing-finding coins-but I believe he's trying" she mentioned to Rebecca on a recent chat between her client sessions. As he closed the door behind them, always locking it despite him living in a safe neighborhood, she engulfed him in passionate kisses. One thing led to another and they found themselves on his living room floor, their shorts pushed down around their ankles, as they couldn't keep their hands off each other. "If vacation is going to be anything like this kind of loving, sign me up!" he excitedly said after he was exasperated with their love-making. They had clearly tapped into an interdependent relationship and traveling to Mexico together would be just one more example of how she had grown and overcome her fears to be more emotionally intimate, or so she felt. The trip will also be the first of its kind in their relationship, and they were prepared for anything.

Two weeks to go before the beach trip and she was beginning to do a pseudo packing type of thing. She would sort through all her vitamins and hair products and face creams that she wanted to take on board the plane. Her status updates on her social networking site were beginning to hint of an upcoming vacation, although she never did like to divulge exactly what she was up to on the social networking blogs, as she always left that up to those who liked to tell everyone every little activity that was happening. She was different. With her passion for nature and witty remarks she kept her "what are you doing?" blurbs to contents relating to Universal and inspirational matters. She did get numerous amounts of "thumbs ups," but she likened it to those curious as to what she was up to and what was coming down the pipe. "Silly ego speaking" she thought while plucking her eyebrows one sunny day. She was writing furiously on a daily basis for several content media sites. She was also working on an eBook, which was a first for her. It wasn't anything fancy or personal, per se, just a small "how to" book on a topic close to her heart. *How to be a Healthy Vegetarian* was the title of choice. The media site that contacted her and asked her to write about this subject knew minimal information about Rachel and her history. It was more of being at the right place at the right time. She got lucky, negotiated a deal with the company who promoted a line of eBooks, and she was able to pick her topic. Not that she was a vegetarian anymore, but eating healthy, being consciously aware of the planet, and writing about it were all dear to her. She devoted many hours each day to the small eBook. It became an all-consuming project for her after the clock-punching hours at the vitamin job. She had to finish it prior to leaving for Mexico, so in her own mind she was sure to relax on vacation. She felt giving him her undivided attention would be bonus for their love life.

More days leading up to their departure date were filled with difficult and challenging interactions between the two of them. "I can't go there anymore" was her continual response when he always wanted to know her whereabouts. "What's up with all the questions?" she again pressed. "Well, if I knew all the answers then I wouldn't have to ask" was his somewhat passive-aggressive rebuttal. There were times the mutual aggravation was so prominent that she hung up on him more often than not because she just couldn't listen to him anymore. "This is going nowhere, and I'm getting cauliflower ear, and you are confusing me!" she raised her voice to him for the umpteenth time. Nothing seemed to make sense or add up in most of their conversations. She called Annabelle to always get her perspective on this most-interesting new path that she and William seemed to be embarking upon. Annabelle would giggle, relate her own stories about her young lover, share her grounded wisdom, and then Rachel was all good for that moment. "Again, just breathe" Annabelle would say when she was spinning out. She was starting to question the meaning of "just breathe" as every time she was on a good flow, he would throw some curveball in her face to test her. It was trying at best. But everything was changing on a spontaneous basis and she never knew what to expect from one moment to the next. If anything he was more consistent than ever; it was Rachel who was bouncing all over the place completely unsure of her decisions and heart. "Shoot, is this what I want?" she asked the pages of her journal, on an evening that William wouldn't give up the good fight.

They were set to leave for Mexico in a matter of a week and they were fighting like cats and dogs only there was no yelling. "I don't want to be with someone who isn't sure of where they are going in life or what they are doing" he said to her while she was discussing possible fun times for the trip. "What does that have to do with Mexico?" she retorted. "I need security" he plainly said, and although she wasn't concerned all that much about money, it wasn't what he was referring to. It was more like emotionally unsettling words that left her feeling unappreciated, disrespected, insulted, and like she didn't have a voice. Despite her ongoing contentment, he seemed determined to knock her off balance with his behavior. "What is going on?" she asked him when they were sitting in his car in the parking lot after purchasing a few cookbooks. He expressed an interest in wanting to learn more about healthy cooking and with her vast experience in that department she accompanied him to the bookstore. "I don't have a clue what you are talking about?" said William in a calm demeanor, which always seemed to infuriate her, as she knew that the more he would act and say something to dissuade the conversation from engaging to downright irritating. "It has to be a planetary thing," she thought to herself while looking out the car window. Typical that her astrology hobby kicked in because it felt like a safe haven to surround herself with at that moment. And with that, she hid her face in her hands and cried in the bookstore parking lot. "What's that all about?" he flippantly asked her. "You have zero sensitivity to who I am" she slobbered into her palms while trying to annunciate her words. "Don't cry now" he genuinely said while attempting to rub her back. "Let's go back to my place, pore over these cookbooks, and come up with some cool dishes to make" he continued while revving up the engine. "Are you kidding me?" "I just want to scream!" which she ended up doing anyway, and about a gazillion decibels louder than the U2 playing on the car radio. He was silent. But then he blurted out "Look, I don't like to yell. My ex-wife yelled all the time. She even threw an iron at me, so I'm trying to avoid some major conflicts here." "You probably deserved it" she profoundly slung back. She was feeling rather mighty with her words. "Is she even your ex yet?" the sensitive topic never quite left her psyche. "We have had all the mediations, the papers are drawn up, and the finale is happening before the year is out" he responded logically. A few long sniffles later, she quietly said "I need to trust my gut." Fortunately, he didn't hear those words and she was rather grateful, as he would have carried that sentence to the utmost of intense conversations, and she just wanted to be quiet. She was definitely sensitive, yet she was also very strong. "Iron fist in the velvet glove," was a phrase she would occasionally say to others if they perceived her to be too weak, given her pleasant and graceful way. On that particular Sunday however, he was getting under her skin the entire day. The Mexico trip was in jeopardy and her gut was in overdrive. She even had shooting abdominal pain whilst they were talking. She also broke down and cried one too many times. "I am totally over-compromising and I AM an incredible person" she said to him while cooking dinner and wanting to validate her own position. She wasn't feeling arrogant at all, quite the opposite. "Damn, I will not be pushed around, controlled, or disregarded for who I am!" she shouted while needing to give herself the reassurance that she had so much to give and it was not in the shape of money or material things. She was a giver of her time and energy. And on that gray afternoon in the college city where they both lived, she was bending way too much to his will.

After she collected herself somewhat she said "I don't feel like helping you learn how to cook." He slightly heard her and responded in a curt manner "fine, I'll order a pizza." Hearing this made her even more furious. "Do you have any idea how junky those things are, and I thought you were trying to be healthy" she blurted out loudly so the neighbors could hear. "What difference does it make?" he commented with glaring eyes. She didn't even look at him, but plainly shouted "look, I'm in no mood to go over anything right now. I have a headache and I just want to go home and be quiet and peaceful." "Good, see you later" he casually said, as if not knowing who she was or what she was about. "Are you serious?" "This kind of interaction is exactly why going to Mexico together is going to be a problemo" was her way of introducing some Spanish into the conversation while still stirring up some drama. "I'm actually not in the mood to talk to you anymore, so you leaving is the best action right now" he responded, which made her even more intent on getting her point across. "You can't just sweep stuff under the carpet." "If we are going to spend our lives together, the least you could do is be more compassionate." He was done. "Okay then, I'm gone." And with those words, she slammed the apartment front door behind her, left the vegetables to find their way back into the refrigerator, and she loaded her pulsating body into the rolling olive. She was drained, again. She was more of a "feeler" and he was more of a "thinker." But, on this evening of supposed cooking and learning togetherness, she ended up alone at her condo reading and he wound up eating some half-ass pizza while watching a basketball game. Both of them were lost in their own worlds, in separate parts of the city.

"Can we make this work and actually have a relaxing vacation by the beach?" she smugly asked him on a walk a few days later, as they both seriously tried to come to some sort of resolution. She was a major talker, and her body language was a bit closed off. She wanted to understand and she was curious, but she wasn't giving in this time. He, on the other hand, would pass off all conversations with a rolling of the eyes, some strange witty remark that didn't even pertain to the topic, and a gouge to her belly just to annoy her. She usually felt worse, never better after his behavior. Their relationship was on a strange track prior to Mexico, and she wanted it to be the beginning of their newfound love.

A clean slate needed to happen. "I feel he has an entirely different agenda pertaining to our relationship, as if there is truly nothing keeping us bonded" she relayed in a text to Annabelle right before bedtime, which kept her tossing and turning all night. She woke up feeling restless. She did some of her own self-foot reflexology in the bathroom, a new regimen she recently adopted after a coworker at the vitamin job suggested it would be a helpful way to ease her foot pain from standing all day. After sitting on the toilet cover for longer than necessary, she approached the mirror, squinted as best she could, applied the essential oils to her chakras, stated her positive intentions, and prepared for her yoga practice. The simple morning routine that started off her day brought her that much-needed peace and joy. She needed to breathe deeply, get him out of her mind for the day, and write. As the hours passed and she thought about their conversations and interaction from the previous days, she couldn't help but apply more essential oil to her heart chakra in the hopes of understanding just what it was keeping them together.

Reminiscing

"Wow, what an incredible vacation to the Caribbean that was!" she found herself telling her nearest and dearest via email the day after they returned from Mexico. So much of the tension prior to leaving had completely dissipated once they set foot on foreign soil. With all the trivialities of customs, flight delays, and bad airport food, they managed to have an amazing ten days together. Not only did they learn about each other in a new and different setting, but their love grew by leaps and bounds. "Spending day in and day out with someone who challenges every fiber of my being is exactly what I needed" she wrote to Annabelle, who she was sure would understand. And it was that daily challenge on all levels of intimacy that launched William and Rachel into a whole new sphere of their relationship. They were now in the throes of real coupledom.

The trip started a bit rocky with their communication, but she likened it to the planet Mercury being in retrograde. She knew after years of astrology being a hobby and primary interest that Mercury retrograde was somewhat hazardous to all things electronic, and just how people's relationships went off the rails with chaos. It spoke volumes on the trip to Mexico. With that information in the back of her mind if there was any tension she would have a wry smile on her lips knowing that the planet was wreaking some havoc on their communication at that moment. He truly understood that she was one of a kind. He mentioned it often in Mexico. He also declared his love for her, despite her having a completely different set of values than he. In fact, he said it was what he loved best about her. She was like no one else in this world, and he was soon coming out of his more logical shell and being completely open with his affections. Holding hands while walking, kissing in public, and constantly caressing her were part of the norm in Mexico. "Um, this is new!" she exclaimed while resting her head on his shoulders on a public bus ride to another part of the beach strip. She loved every minute of it, as this public display of affection was not in his DNA at all, but after ten days at the beach with nary a care in the world he wanted that very world to know how he felt about his woman. They were mirrors of each other. They were both transforming and growing in ways that astounded them and even friends and coworkers. Their Imago relationship was in full swing. There were no exits. "What is an Imago?" she asked him one day. "Sounds like some Italian sauce or cheese" she seriously asked him. "It is where two people are images of each other," he stated in a teacher-kind-of-mode. "I learned about it years ago in therapy with my ex, although we had no indications of being in that type of scenario with our marriage." "I don't want to mention her, if that's cool" she responded in a very confident way. "Good" he said. "We aren't on this trip to go over the past." "I would like to think we are here to get some rays, relax, have some fun, and explore a bit" he chimed in rather confidently himself.

Every morning in the hotel she would wake up before he even had a chance to roll over and put his arms around her, catch the morning sunrise from their balcony overlooking the ocean, stroll down to the nearest coffee joint, grab both of them a hot tea, then meander back to the room only to have him stumbling around in the bathroom after rousing up from his slumber and wiping the sleep from his eyes. She liked to get up early. He enjoyed sleeping in. The morning ritual for the entire time they were in Mexico was easy and it worked for both of them. They didn't have much early morning banter, so the flow of their routines just naturally fell into place until it was time for yoga. He wasn't much of the yoga devotee that she had become, but he was willing to give it a try while they were away on vacation. Staying in a hotel at the ocean's door was the perfect setting for him to begin a practice that never seemed to get off the ground back in their college city. He was an intense guy. He was wrapped up in his own competitive nature of exercise and it never bothered her one bit. She knew his true self and the mere fact that he expressed a daily interest in yoga surprised and pleased her. "If anything, it might help him sleep better" her subconscious cropped up and surmised.

They would set up their oversized towels on a small grass patch facing the ocean. It was far better than getting sand all over their sweaty bodies and dealing with every tourist walking around them chattering about their previous night's drunken stupor. Both of them didn't imbibe in hard alcohol, so people recovering from a hangover certainly got no sympathy from them. Doing yoga on the grass patch that was mere steps from the sand would suffice. It had been awhile since she taught a private yoga class. Having him alongside her and following her every move while she calmly guided him through the poses gave her a very serene feeling. As they breathed through each pose with the ocean waves hitting the shore in front of them, the world just seemed right. He wasn't that flexible, but he sure gave it his best. "Hmmm, is that a metaphor for who he is?" she thought as she stood in warrior pose. She provided the visuals, easy instruction, and meditation at the end of the session. Both of them would sit on their towels, face the ocean, hear nothing but birds and waves, a few voices in the background, and all was well. They would sit in this auspicious silence long enough to surrender to the day and be grateful for each moment. They would then gather their towels place them on a lounge chair by the pool for the hotel maintenance people to collect at the end of the day, and saunter to the beach to walk from one end of the stretch of hotels to the other. They rarely spoke for the first few minutes after yoga, as nothing needed to be said. Somehow the morning was a rare processing time for both of them, but they were able to do it interdependently. Once either one of them spoke while on the long walk in the sand their only words were "are you ready to turn around?" and with that, they would face the oncoming winds and make their way back to the hotel for the complimentary buffet breakfast.

After a few days and feeling settled into their temporary environs, they had a few conflicts that arose leaving the other rather wounded. As much as she wanted to just throw in the towel something deep inside of her kept her in the game, being challenged and learning. "I sometimes have to take a stance and not give up who I am by succumbing to his words all the time" she emailed Annabelle in a private social media message. She wasn't even sure he knew that that was the case. She wasn't a big fan of conflict, but she certainly was able to handle it, not cry, not get angry, but simply not react, and instead, take about a hundred big deep breaths. She just never gave up. Their fights were usually so trivial anyway, but it cut to the core of who they were now. One evening while they were sort of relaxing and pushing each other's buttons again, he decided to leave the room, go down to the lounge where the nightly singers were crooning their best Temptations' hits, and she would emerge into some type of pseudo slumber, whereby her back was facing the door and it sure seemed like she was angry. "Seriously?" "This is all such a game of hearts" she quietly said to herself in the mirror while washing her sun-worn face after a full day of shelling. He was already in the lobby stewing on his own stuff, so the minute he exited the room, she remembered that her face was still scrappy from the day, and with all their mirroring, she forgot to wash it. It felt like a game to her, but she had already gazed at the vast array of stars from the balcony, said her nightly spiritual mantras, and going to bed was the only other option. When he returned she pretended to be asleep so as to not give him the satisfaction of rehashing the conflict they had in the first place. She was simply grateful he returned to the room and didn't swallow his pride in some tequila bottle.

"The reason this trip is so perfect is that it isn't perfect," he proclaimed one day while they were tanning themselves to a crisp on the chairs plopped in the sand. "Well, that's a pretty profound statement given all our words of late" she turned to face him from the lounge chairs. It was a windy day and both of them were determined to make the most of the ten days on vacation, so they withstood wind, lots of cloud coverage, nearby cigarette smoke, a few spring break partiers sprinkled in for good measure, and waves so big it was impossible to swim in the ocean. They resorted to lying out and relaxing for a few hours on the first day then decided to hit the town and get some basic sundries for the remainder of their stay. Even though he was the financial wizard of the two, they were both on a tight budget and staying at a four-star resort was taxing them to the max. He was gracious enough to use his immense amount of saved-up rewards points for the duration at the hotel, but they both had to fend for themselves with respect to daily nourishment. She more than obliged, as she wanted them to be on equal footing. She learned her lesson from the past that no man will own her, control her, or do more than his fair share with her. "I have to exchange some dollars for pesos" seemed to be the daily communication on how they were to afford resort living.

The next morning she began a customary habit of doing her solo meditation, sitting quietly on the toilet lid, rubbing the essential oils on her chakras, then venturing down to the lobby of the hotel to retrieve two hot teas for her and William. What struck her as so interesting is that she was perfectly comfortable meditating in the bathroom with the door closed while sitting on the edge of the bathtub. "Good thing I have some extra cushion on my ass because going from the toilet seat to the porcelain tub kind of makes me laugh" she wrote in her journal that morning. Since he wasn't much of a sound sleeper throughout the night, she felt any chance he had to get some rest would not only help him and any irritability the following day, but it gave her some alone time in the morning. Choosing the beautifully tiled tub's edge with lights off was the perfect scenario for her. She continued to be a simple woman. At her menopausal stage of life not much seemed to upset her; only perhaps the occasional times she would run out of dark chocolate. "I need that stuff to alter my mood every day" she surmised to herself, and even others at the vitamin job. She knew enough about nutrition to attest to the benefits of dark chocolate.

She quietly left the room, walked the six flights of stairs down to the lobby, people buzzing all around, preparing themselves for a day of leisure by the ocean or the immensely intricate resort pool. The local women at the gift shop recognized her as a regular, pouring the hot water in the paper cup, doubling up on the sleeve that surrounds the cup so as not to burn her hands for the return back up six flights of stairs to the room. "I am so loving all this exercise just to get a few cups of tea!" she raised her voice excitedly to a few tourists waiting for the elevator. After a few days she wouldn't even take any money to buy the teas. The women at the register simply asked for her room number and she would leave the gift shop with two green teas, a Snickers bar for William, and a dark chocolate bar for herself. It was their daily breakfast on a budget, and it worked to rouse them into the morning for another ritual of yoga and long walks on the beach in the deep white sand.

The Groove Lounge

They spent every day in that manner. "I want to take a few shells back home, if we find some cool ones" he said on one of their early beach walks. With that both their heads turned their gazes downward, and they were fixated on finding unique shells to carry back home. The pelicans nose-diving in the distance, the ocean rumbling in their ears, the faint sounds of people's voices as they passed, she managed to spot a large ruffled-looking shell. It was the catch of the day. A pinkish-beige conch that was partially buried in the sand caught her attention. Conch shells were not rare; it's just that they got scooped up quickly if spotted on the beach. The local men would always pass by their beach chairs and try to sell these shells to all the tourists who were silly enough to buy them. She couldn't help but feel sorry for these local people walking by every minute, peddling their wares in Spanish. She thought of their families and how even making one dollar that day would make a difference in their lives. But finding a conch shell on her own made her forget about all that. She carried that heavy shell back to their room, along with a few other straggler designer shells of all shapes and sizes. She emptied the bag onto the table on their deck and sorted through all their finds. "How are we going to take all these back to the states and not pay more for bag weight?" said William being his logical and practical self. "Maybe we could leave the duplicates behind and focus on the unique ones" she answered his question, trying to be logical herself.

The maid had been to their room, cleaned and organized their belongings, leaving them with fresh tiny bottles of shampoo, lotion, and body wash. The fresh towels were neatly folded inside the porcelain tub/shower shelf, the new robes were hung, cool tempo music playing in the background, and the corner of the bed turned down to resemble the shape of an envelope. The maid also left a locally made sweet treat on the pillow, which was difficult for both of them to decipher. They had already committed to drinking the water, as it proclaimed to be filtered, but that little tampon-looking dessert looked ominous, and they ended up trashing it with no guilt. "The music and ambiance is so getting me in the mood" he mumbled as he put his arms around her waist and pulled her in close. They had already showered after a full day of shelling, body surfing, more beach walking, and classic dinners at offbeat places. Every day they hit the sack tired and more in love than ever. Only that particular evening he seemed to listen more closely to the music in the room. The maid had left them with their T.V. piping in a very groovy series of tunes that felt straight out of a romance novel. There were no lyrics; just a throbbing and pumping of beats that got him going.

"Whoa, this is new!" she exclaimed as she plopped onto the bed with her new sundress a bit disheveled after he was getting in the mood. They had already been registered as guests at the resort for a few days, yet the turn-down that the maid provided every evening was certainly a sight for sore eyes and music to their ears. He joined her on the bedside, but started to get rather horny, and he wasn't one to hide his need for connecting with her when it came to the loins. He just found her so damn sexy all the time that he felt showing her in physically intimate ways was the most profound connection. She had a habit of feeling uneasy at first. With the groove music playing in the background, the sliding glass door open, the ocean breeze lightly blowing the thin linen drapes, he pulled her sundress up to her chest and began stroking her belly. She got chill bumps, as this light touch sent a shiver up her spine because she knew what was coming next. He was an awesome lover. He had a way of making her come about four to five times each love-making session, and the time in Mexico was no different. They were both slathered in sweat by the time their bodies melted into one lump on the mattress. "I love to try new things on vacation and my god honey, you gave me more reasons than ever to take notes!" she proclaimed to him while he lay motionless on the bed, and she was in the comfy robe on the balcony looking at the stars. The night was as black as ever, and the formation of Jupiter, Venus, the Big Dipper, and all the other celestial beings were shining brightest in the sky. "Perhaps it's because we can't see all of them in our light-polluted college city" she said to him, as he was still looking worn out on the sheets after a very long and engaging lovemaking session. She didn't dwell in bed too long. She liked to get up, move around, and talk a lot. He felt the only sleep he was afforded was after their lovemaking. He only felt tired after he pumped and grinded and spanked her until they both experienced ecstasy at the same time. It was a first for them. "I think you might have cracked my neck back into a normal state" she mentioned to him when he finally got up, put a robe on, and joined her on the balcony. The positions that they found themselves in during the hour plus long session was heavy with so much newness that neither one of them felt they could remember what exactly transpired. He was in the moment of sex. He had Rachel on her back, her legs straddling God knows what, using his lips, his hands, his words, and his very well-endowed member to give her screams of pleasure. She returned the favor in kind, by talking dirty, stroking every inch of his well-muscled body, and taking charge every now and again during the hour. It was what he had wanted all along, and because of this newfound intimacy taking place, both of them weren't holding back. If anything they set the bar so high that reaching bliss each and every time was virtually impossible. "I was so in the moment, I can't imagine having that kind of time to explore our bodies in those kinds of ways again" she told him silently on the rough plane ride home. He softened his eyes and forehead, sat back in the narrow plane seat, had a smile on his lips, leaned into her and said "I love you." She uttered the words "and I have loved you for years." Both of them had truly proclaimed their commitment to each other. Through years of their friendship, complications with exes, new beginnings in different states, ill-fated soul connections, and the one trip to Mexico, they had sealed their love for each other. "Only this time, it's real." She told all her best girlfriends. She had the support of every single one of them, all happy and excited knowing that she was patient, persistent, wise, and so very much an independent spirit. She had sent them all photos of her and William out to dinner a few nights in the tropical paradise. Both of them looked relaxed and refreshed. A few friends commented that "he looks so grounded." This gave her the impetus to truly think how different they were. She was the creative spontaneous spirit. He was the logical and grounded one.

Returning to their college city after ten days in the Caribbean sparked an interdependent streak in both of them. They talked about spending more time together. He had requested that they see each other more than once per week, and she willingly obliged. After a relatively short and bump-free flight to their home destination, they trudged through the airport parking lot with more weight in their bags, given the amount of shells they carted home and no extra bag fees. "Thank god" he said to the reservationist weighing his bag one last time. In one of her old behavior OCD modes back at the resort, she managed to throw away a very crucial piece of immigration paper that was necessary to board the flight. The lines were out the door, she didn't have any more money on her, and they only took cash. She gave him some puppy dog eyes and he willingly helped her out to get her on the plane to the states. "No worries at all" he whispered to her as he was fumbling for wads of cash that the immigration attendant demanded. She was more than grateful, promised to pay him back (since they were willingly on equal terms), and all was well.

They didn't say much on the car ride back to his apartment. It was just understood that they would spend one more night together at his place before they resumed their separate and independent lives. They were both tired, hungry, and spewed out a few memorable moments of the trip. "Remember that bus ride in the rain where the driver wouldn't let you off in time, and you practically jumped out the door?" William laughed so hard saying this, which got Rachel reminiscing as well. "That was hilarious" she piped in. "And the array of interesting people on the bus made it that much more fun" she continued. "When we got to the hotel, soaking wet, and that big old booger that was hanging out your nose like a maggot!" she doubled over that moment in laughter just thinking about it. "Oh my god, you didn't even tell me it was there, and I was walking past so many people that evening in the lobby" he chuckled back to her. "I know, that's what made it great" she hugged him and they both continued to have gut-aches with laughter over that funny incident in Mexico.

After they arrived to their hometown, the thick, humid air, cooler temperatures, and concrete highways paled in comparison to where they both had just been. The moon wasn't even visible high in the sky. Nothing felt the same anymore. The transformation that was taking place was not just Rachel alone. It was William undergoing his own process as well.

Coins on the Road

or as long as she could remember she was a lucky person. Most events or life changes she would simply dream about, yet deep down she knew that they would all come true. She had a way of making things happen. On one particular balmy morning, with the Spring Equinox on the horizon, she started ramping up her motives and aspirations. Her writing was taking center stage now, and so much of her being was wrapped up in creative inspiration and moving forward with her purpose in mind. Hearts appeared etched in the pavement on her walks, tiny birds perched on the branches in trees with big fat voices, yellow and orange and white butterflies flying all around her every time she set foot out the door, and one lucky penny, dime, or nickel after another to solidify that angels were guiding her throughout this phase of her life.

He was away on a four-day spiritual retreat for the weekend, and she had the drive to write as often and as much as possible. The vitamin job was only a means to keep a roof over her head and pay some crucial bills that always demanded her attention. Her heart and passion was in the written word. As they were blending their lives more and more each day he even mentioned to her "you can bring your computer over to my house and write from here" was how he phrased it while both she and he were relaxing with their faces in the sun. "Hmmm, that would be cool." "Then I wouldn't miss a beat of the ongoing creativity swooping in on me right now" she said trying to sound like her idol Hemingway, or some other famous author. She had just returned from a run around the lake, watched the ducks gliding on the water, the koi occasionally jumping with a freshly caught insect in their mouth, and nobody around to interfere with her Zen. Running always gave her the impetus to process thoughts for the day. She thought about her conversation with him that morning. She had small affirmations that she professed to the nearby trees in the woods, as she strongly bounded on the trail doing many laps around the lake to keep the creative juices flowing. She profoundly pondered how they took yet another leap forward in their intimacy by exploring previous taboo subjects and actions. It was exactly what she needed to take a step in the direction of her ultimate destiny. She was so locked into fear mode when it came to his forthright sexual and romantic behavior. He just always found her to be hot, and he even wanted to take her right then and there after her sweaty run. "I probably smell pretty bad" was her way of making excuses for her low libido. "You always smell good to me." "I don't recall a time when you've ever smelled bad" he responded somewhat knowing her excusive behavior. He cornered her in the laundry room as she was getting the ingredients from the pantry to make her post-exercise green drink. At first she was reluctant. But he looked so damn hot that particular morning; all scruffy and shirtless and a wonderful musty smell from his own exercise session earlier. She couldn't resist, and the two of them found themselves having another physically-charged session on the kitchen floor, leaving them both in a pool of sweat and exhaustion. "I know you have to get going, but I just wanted to tell you how much I enjoyed the past few days with you, the dinner you cooked, the walks we took together, and the incredible trust you felt for me during our love-making last night" he said as he gave her one last hug before she headed out the door to go punch a clock. She agreed that she had never been so open and vulnerable with any man before. She had never been one to be very vocal during sex, but something about him and his sensual ways had her transforming in her own right. Her emotional repressions felt like they were lifting. She might have even screamed on a climatic session. "It was all such a blur again" she thought so dreamily.

She drove home, sat at her computer, and wrote and wrote. Not only was he a supportive force for her writing passion, but he was helping her network within the writing community, and giving her the impetus and inspiration to feel creative. She had always said that the ocean and vastness made her experience more deeply the joy and expressions of words on paper, yet every time they had been together since the Mexico trip, her writing was spilling over into emails to friends, her own simple blog, small stories on social networking sites, and lots of pages devoted to her second novel. He was well-connected, albeit humbly, and he would suggest people to contact for her to get her words out there. She had already authored and published her first novel when they were in the throes of their initial meeting, and she welcomed any help from him when it came to her craft.

He was exploring his own career changes as well, so she in turn, had some righteous connections that could jump start him on his new path. "With our mutual direction we could certainly take this path together and grow even more and learn even more" was her rational side coming out when lying side by side after a love-making session.

She woke up the next morning with a severe headache; one she hadn't experienced since before they were together. She slept in her own condo after a long eight-hour day at the vitamin job, her feet aching and throbbing, and her eyes burning and sore from staring at a large computer most of the day. "No wonder I have a headache" she mentioned to the lavender candle she was lighting for the morning. She had two very poignant dreams that caused her insides to turn and her subconscious to feel weird. Both dreams involved interesting endings. The first dream showed a very large black bear in the woods, who wasn't necessarily pursuing her, but she was aware of its presence. Soon a man appeared and shot the bear after she had pleaded with him to let it be. The image of the bear lying on the ground with a bullet wound to its belly caused her so much grief that she found herself crying uncontrollably over a sink. "That was a disturbing dream." she thought as she rolled over to the other side of her awesome pillow. The second dream was a praying mantis that seemed a bit larger than normal and bit her on her finger while she was sitting outside in the sun. She shook off the unique insect that led into the next scene whereby the praying mantis turned into a sweet puppy dog sitting at the glass door waiting to come in. "Wow, I have to look up these dreams to know what's going on with my subconscious!" she nervously pondered as the dream dictionary book stared her in the face begging to be open. She researched the meaning of the two poignant dreams, sat back in her somewhat uncomfortable desk chair, and stared at the computer screen that made her brain go on overdrive. Then the phone rang, and her caller I.D. said "William Jameson."

"I was hoping we could spend some time together today" he spoke in his most beautiful and soft voice. He wasn't one to raise his voice or get angry. If anything, he would walk away from confrontation, or put another wad of chew in the side of his mouth, or sit at his own computer and stare. "I have to punch the clock today, and I'm not terribly happy about it" she responded in a rather abrupt and strong voice. She was coming into her own. The lovely water dreams she used to have years ago have been replaced by simple messages from the angels that were giving her a heads up. At least that's what she though all the crazy dreams were about. The cosmos were in somewhat of a planetary upheaval and she was doing her best to keep her head above water, balancing the vitamin job, William, her writing, the daily tasks and nuances that brought her joy, and moving forward with her purpose. One thing was clear, she was going through the change of life. She had enough know-how to understand that the extremely heavy period she experienced for the entire month of October basically set her up to be in full-blown menopause. He professed to understand the ramifications of her new phase of life, yet as she experienced one hot flash after another, many sweaty sleepless nights, irritability, and more confidence in her opinions and words, he felt like he was moving down the list. It was a feeling he was not so keen on, as his previous wife always left him in somewhat of a pile on the floor.

"I found a dime, two quarters, and a few pennies this week!" he said happily, as he and Rachel were walking a friends' dog in the neighborhood. "Wow, that's cool" her face tried to be happy, but she knew that the coin finds were her thing. She took on numerous dog-sitting jobs on the side to keep things real in her life. It also afforded her extra money during the month for those pedicures and massages she always managed to etch out time for in her life. Even him professing that he found some coins in random places gave her pause. It was her thing. She always found lucky pennies and the occasional dime in fun and new places. It seemed that every time she would just glance down at the ground there was a coin strategically placed there for her to pick up. She knew her angels were guiding her. Either that or someone repeatedly dropped coins for her to pick up. At first she was bothered by him even mentioning his coin finds. "This is my thing, and it's who I am" she retorted to him while the friend's dog was pulling hard on the leash to smell everything and anything. As much as she was attracted to William and all his differing opinions and behaviors, she certainly didn't want to share her serendipitous coin finds that seemed so personal. "Is this a God wink merging our lives for us?" she wondered while gazing at the extremely blue sky and brisk air, thinking about the interdependence that she was now involved in with him. He was doing lots of soul work, gads of transforming, and plenty of emotional upheaval actions to warrant finding a coin or two on the road. The world wasn't just her playground anymore, or so she thought. She was moving slowly with her newfound relationship with him, yet her heart was thrust into noticing more synchronistic events with him. She couldn't sit on the sidelines and wait for things to happen. She had to get in the game, take more steps forward, and visualize an amazing life with him that she had never seen before. He was already two steps ahead of her in the dream meaning, and she continued to scratch her head as to how this all happened and where they were within their seemingly perfect dynamic.

Twin Souls

Silliness prevailed in their togetherness. It's as if they were both children trapped in adult bodies, playing out one movie after another, and constantly laughing so hard until their guts were about to burst. Since she was in her mid-fifties, and he was about nine years younger, she was dubbed the "cougar" within her circle of friends. She passed the comments and remarks off as just another different way she chose to live her life. "I still have that rebellious streak and wild side" she intimated to her Mom on the routine monthly chat. "Don't you think a man your own age would be more preferable?" her mother asked in sort of a been-there-done-that tone. "Nah, I've been there and look how it turned out" she replied. "Okay then, just make sure he knows what he's in for" her mom answered in her usual passive-aggressive way. "We're all good, Mom. No need to worry." "I love you and will talk in a few weeks" she said calmly, as if knowing her own conversations with her mother showed significant growth on her behalf. They were finally on the same page.

When out to dinner one evening at an exclusive restaurant both of them decked out in their best outfits and treated themselves to a nice dining experience. After they had ordered quality appetizers, dinner, and even a crème brulee for dessert, she stepped outside of her formal etiquette ways and blew her nose in the ecru linen napkin, right there at the dinner table. "That's not a nose napkin!" he blurted out in the dimly lit restaurant. The two of them were laughing so uncontrollably that tears were streaming down their faces, and their dinners felt as though they were on the verge of being refunded from their stomachs. The nearby dining patrons didn't bat an eye, and even so, she wouldn't have cared. She was just being her carefree self. She was silly, childlike, fun, happy, and so eager to learn new things all the time. He finally understood what she was all about, and despite the lack of class she exhibited at that moment in the fine dining restaurant, it was the constant laughter and forever memories of their silliness that kept his heart on fire. He tended to lean towards a more serious nature, but she had a way of keeping him light and airy, yet still true to himself. She abhorred people who weren't authentic to themselves. It confused her and seemed sad. She could never understand how anyone would want to mimic another in how they live their lives and who they chose to hang out with every day. Whenever he copied her with a behavior that she knew was a deviation from his true self, she would call him out on it. He did the same to her. They were two souls now traveling on the same path.

Work was picking up for Rachel. She was balancing more hours at the vitamin job, writing more and expressing herself creatively, and picking up extra side dog-sitting jobs just because it gave her joy and unconditional companionship. Since she had an inherent wanderlust spirit, the dog jobs were a means to satisfy her craving for always wanting to get up and go. Staying at other people's homes, caring for their animals, walking them in nature, playing with them on the bed and various couches, she was quite literally in dog heaven. She hadn't been with a full time dog for a few years since the passing of her beloved Labrador, so spending quality time with a variety of breeds and temperaments was helping her with the transition of wanting a dog again. Since he was a dog lover himself the two of them would settle on a dog together someday. "He is so great with dogs' she wrote in her journal one day. "I remember him telling me he taught his dog to bring in the mail every day, walk perfectly off-leash, and go down the slide at the nearby playground" she continued to pen it in her notes. He spoke "dog" to them, cooing, flubbing his jowls, getting low in their space, and rubbing his muzzle against theirs. Every time she witnessed that behavior it was clear they were both meant to be. Despite their early roller coaster ride of a relationship they had evolved to such solid growing intimacy that even their harmonious flatulence began to make sense. Shyness from the onset paved the way for complete and total honesty with their bodies, minds, and souls.

"It certainly is no ordinary life," she calmly said to one of her coworkers. At the vitamin job she again felt as though something bigger was happening underneath her feet. It could have been that one of her older peers at the job was doing her best to undermine whatever it was that she was doing. She only punched the clock three or four days per week, yet whenever she set foot in the old, stark, and fluorescently lit building, she instantly felt a sense of oppression and claustrophobia. All her creative inspiration from her morning routine of listening to the birds, the sun in her face, going for a long walk or run, launching into strenuous and invigorating yoga positions, and making her bed (which she found strangely satisfying); it all got lost in the mundaneness of the vitamin job. She kept reminding herself the work was a means to keep a roof over her head until the big break, but she always hoped that the bright spot to her hours at the store was having fun, being who she was, and tasking at her job. The store was a busy place. A constant stream of people came in from the moment the doors opened, needing pills and advice every hour to cure whatever ailed them. It did give all the employees the feeling of gratitude to have a job in tough economic times. The neediness and energy of it all drained Rachel. She loved to help people, but she also felt that more than half of them had to take some responsibility for their lives. "A pill isn't the cure-all," she would often whisper to a fellow coworker.

The first part of each shift at the store went by rather quickly. She had a groove that she got into and it flowed. The disruption of that flow and everyone else's around her was the arrival of one worker who was fairly new. The new person, Josie, had a wonderful heart, lots of emotional damage (Rachel could spot that right away), and seemed to be a know-it-all, but only around Rachel. "Why does she butt in during one of my mini-consultations with a customer?" she thought to herself every single time it happened. The energy of the store shifted whenever Josie arrived. Something felt off. She was intuitive enough to know that things just didn't feel right. She had that praying mantis dream, after all. "Could this woman be the devil in disguise?" was her subconscious doing a number on every shift they worked together . She knew that Josie was a good person, but not necessarily a team player. It was just tough to be around all that for eight hours at a time. Deep in the back of her mind was the presence of her creative writing and how her craft and passion was about to take center stage. She would daydream during the slow times at the vitamin job about how many pages she could be churning out. Despite the off-energy she felt from Josie she still knew she had to be responsible enough to pay her bills every month. "My big breakthrough is happening as we speak" was her daily voice beckoning inside the walls of her ever-present mind. She walked to the back hallway, found her punch card, and slid it under the clock to get paid for the hours she accounted for that day. She left the fluorescent lights, the low dirty ceiling, the constant stream of needy people, and Josie behind for another day. The bright spot came when William called to talk about his spiritual sessions with his mentor. He was on the most incredible path for his own transformation, and as tired as her feet were after standing on concrete floors all day and listening to one whine after another, the sound of his soft and tender voice made her smile and relax. She was, once again, inspired.

Both of them felt a bit empty after they encountered each other for more than a few days, more so when they went their separate ways and returned to their own independent lives, albeit simple and meaningful, but they couldn't wait to see each other again. The reunions happened at his apartment, as he had the bigger place, a lake nearby to take an evening walk, quality tennis courts, higher ceilings, and that immensely pleasing king size mattress. She enjoyed her own space at home every once in a while, yet staying at his place gave her more tranquility than ever. It was a far cry from the Rachel of earlier days, whereby she needed her space almost hourly after she encountered him. The intensity was just too much. Their chemistry was so prevalent that it transcended all else. They were merging their lives and the emotions that accompanied that merger were ever present. She was beginning to "out" herself on social networking sites. She was one to always keep a low profile, yet her close friends knew that she had been through years of struggle and reparation. She felt so validated when they liked her recent photos of the Yucatan peninsula. "I haven't posted any photos of William and I just yet, but that is the next step" she texted her best girlfriend in Colorado. She even mentioned to him that she was going to let the world know who her twin soul was and how their parallel lives were in the beginnings of a merger. All of her repressed emotions were now bubbling up. The dreams were more prominent, synchronicities were apparent every day, and she had never felt more confident and attractive.

As they went for an evening walk around the lake after dinner, holding hands now in their usual public-display-of-affection manner, he began to open up more about past events of his life. "Wow, I didn't even know that happened to you!" she said to him, but also knowing that the same type of event happened to her at around the same time in her own life. For him to discuss details of his previous life through his two marriages, she again felt a sense of closeness to him.

Not only did he begin to do her laundry and grocery shop for them, he invited her into his world each and every day. He was on a sabbatical of sorts, and completely in a newfound way of relating to her, and doing his life. His weekly schedule wasn't caught up in corporate life any more. He was getting his hands on every spiritual book he could find, reading it to the end in a few days, jotting down notes, getting inspired, wanting to talk to her about the contents, and basically waking up to a new mindset. As the days and weeks progressed they began to carve out more time together. Whenever she had to be on a dog-sitting job for any length of time she made sure that she would see him prior to the dates. She would cook for them, he would give her a home massage, complete with professional oils and whatnot, she scrubbed his back in the shower, he would arrange for her oil to be changed in her car, and they both would sit on his deck with the sun in their faces for hours on end. Their lives were one big blended symphony. Despite the fact that she was balancing three different jobs, two of them being her major passions, she put him on the front burner. She had never done that before with any lover or husband, and it made her think how much his presence had furthered her own growth. He became a very appreciative soul and respected her efforts more than ever. "I think you are going to be an incredibly successful writer" he would always mention to her, in either email or on the phone. "Thanks babe. I'm trying" she humbly responded, as to not let it go to her head. He was her biggest fan and supporter. Even though he was going through his own contemplation of where his career was headed, he managed to protect Rachel, take care of her in the most subtle ways, and be the best lover she had ever had. The earth literally moved every time they made love. Their intimacy became deeper and more evolved and it only made the connection in bed that much better. She wasn't much of a talker in the bedroom, but she learned to ask for what she needed. Her shyness and modesty gave way to a more sexually confident woman. He was thrilled with this physical transformation, yet he knew in his heart that she had it in her all along. It is why he was initially attracted to her. "From the moment I saw you sitting on that big blue Fit ball at the gym, I knew you were fun, happy, sexy, and quite an interesting woman" he said to her one day in the grocery store while they were shopping from their new cookbook. She just smiled, put some extra dark chocolate in the basket, and calmly walked away with a sassy spring to her step.

Synchronicities were in full swing for Rachel. "Just as I was wishing there was a bit more of the color red in my life a cardinal bird appears out of nowhere on my run this morning!" she excitedly told him, as he was writing out his affirmations while sitting in the sun on the deck. He smiled and continued his peace and relaxation. He, himself, had just returned from a full-throttle exercise session at his local gym, and had the scrapes, bruises, and sore shoulders to prove it. Both of them valued health and exercise as number one in their lives. Their meals were uncomplicated and full of color and goodness. "I'll do the cooking, and you can do the shopping" she confidently told him as he was applying some antiseptic to his latest open exercise wound. He wanted more of her time. He was not settling for a part-time relationship any more. His previous marriage that was still quite fresh in his mind gave him the impetus to be more vulnerable with his feelings and he continued to let her know what he needed. At first she was always on the defensive, as she never wanted another man to control her, or cross the boundaries she had set for herself, but she was a wise and tough woman, or so she thought. He had a way of maneuvering the conversation to make it seem as though she had the upper hand. She didn't, of course. They were on equal pages, yet he still had some major insecurities lingering that she wanted so much to understand, but found herself just wanting space. "I feel like I've gone through three years of personal growth and now I'm learning how to apply that knowledge to this relationship" she told him while stretching on his deck. "I get that, but I still want to see you more than once or twice per week" he responded rather seriously. It never failed. Ever since they returned from their nirvana Mexico vacation, he would insert the "I need to see you more" comment, which was a turn-off for her and she needed to understand why.

Their twin soul relationship was filled with drama. It was never an easy one. If anything, it presented more challenges and obstacles than a regular old boring union of two people. Their twin flame had dynamic and heart. She read somewhere that "The twin flames can undergo several stages of their partnership." She was feeling as though they were about to enter into the "runner stage", whereby one partner feels the need to run away from the intensity of the union to savor their growth for a bit then reunite when both twins souls have completed their karma. They were both running. They were mirroring each other to a major degree. It all happened so abruptly, but something had felt off for her ever since they returned from Mexico. He was on sabbatical, exploring his own stuff, and not wanting to do it alone. She, on the other hand, had spent three solo years of her own growth, moving around from one city to the next, in the hopes of gaining some reasons and closure as to why her soul was dictating all the directions she was taking. He pays people to help him with his soul work. He had oodles of books, mentors, and philosophers at his beck and call to aid in his understanding of what his soul needed. She admired his tenacity, supported his efforts, and felt like she needed to sit back and allow whatever was happening to happen. They had been forcing the relationship lately, and it didn't feel right to either of them. She was sensing the need to run. He provoked her on all levels, and both of them knew that love was present at the deepest core of their beings. She just needed some space.

Wanderlust

She was such a nomad at heart. Days of dog sitting jobs were coming in more frequently and she found herself satisfying her indulgences for luxury, travel, and giving through hanging out with cool dogs, being in a new neighborhood in her own college city, and having the ability to write and raid the fridge. She had been lucky enough to land some well-connected clients, who trusted her implicitly with their dogs and cats. She loved spending time with each animal, creating a fun environment, following the directions that were given by each owner, although she usually deviated a bit from the explicit instructions given. "I'm not good at setting house alarms, so we'll just lock up and trust all will be okay" she would happily mention to each dog before exiting on a walk. When she left each home with satisfied and tired animals, it made her feel as though it was a job well done. It also squelched her constant need to uproot, travel, explore, and take an adventure in other places that called her name. For that moment, she was not feeling the need to move to another city any time soon. Her relationship with William was giving her reasons to grow, learn, and have one of the greatest love stories ever. But caring for others' animals was the best way she could feel the immediate balance of her inner being. She was able to continue writing, she was giving back, and she was surrounded by the most upgraded domesticity she could not possibly afford on her own at a crucial stage of her life. Giving up the real estate profession way back when was tough for her, but she knew that her purpose was much less chaotic and more down-to-earth. As she juggled the vitamin job, her creative writing, the dog-sitting gigs, and William, she definitely needed to take a time out. With him wanting more togetherness time and her clients traveling more, plus the vitamin job asking for more hours, she was appreciative of the getaways in luxurious environments. The dogs were happy. The owners were grateful and she satisfied her wanderlust spirit. It was a win/win situation.

One morning she had planned to plop herself on her yoga mat and launch into a serene meditation. "I know these dogs want to play every time I hit the floor, but they are going to have to wait for just a bit" she looked up to the heavens and said to God. God had another plan altogether. The two beagles were demanding her attention, dropping every possible chewy toy and stuffed animal on her yoga mat to alert her to their presence, and she soon forgot her own needs, leashed them up, and off she went, both of them dragging her down the street.

One of the dogs was about seven years younger than the other and had so much uncontrollable energy that she was constantly pulling on the leash to show she had a little alpha dog control in her. It wasn't her usual theme as her arm was being stretched to the max, the dog was gasping for air, and she felt as though she was choking the poor animal. She also had to remain aware of the older beagle who basically didn't need a leash. She decided to unhook the older dogs' leash and let her just trail behind them on the walk. It worked for a while until a squirrel crossed their path and both hounds took off. Only the younger one was on a leash and she didn't want to deny the animal some freedom so she unhooked its leash as well. There were other people around in the neighborhood walking their own dogs on and off leash. One couple could tell that the dogs did not belong to her, so they offered to help round them up should they get too far out of sight. The older dog stayed close to her and came when called. The younger dog was on a mission. Every smell, sound, or movement-that wild dog went bonkers for the freedom she was provided, and decided to take off up hills and cliffs. She was about to lose her mind. She thought "if I lose this dog or something bad happens to it, I'll feel so horrible and irresponsible" said her random rational subconscious. The couple who were walking in proximity to the action helped her corral the younger dog back. Fortunately, the older dog just followed Rachel on her quest to direct and cajole the younger beagle to return to their presence. It felt like it took a village. Her heart skipped about a thousand beats for as long as the little hound was not in sight. She even had a few hot flashes, which usually happened when she was stressed. Then the young pup appeared out of nowhere, she hooked her back up on the extended leash, at least giving her a little more freedom for the walk home, and her whole body was no longer shaking. She thanked the couple for helping her do a mild search for the precocious beagle, and once back to the luxurious mansion on the hill, she gave them both treats, fresh water, and watched as they slunk on the couch in sheer exhaustion. In her usual non-alpha dog fashion she said "good doggies, you two are the best!" and sat next to them stroking their tired and pulsating bellies.

The weekend came to an end and she had just about played with each dog, throwing the various assortments of squeaky toys until her arm almost fell off. The dogs were definitely tuckered out. In her typical way she left a lengthy synopsis for the owners regarding the events of the weekend with their "children". She always wanted to reassure the owners that the pups were well taken care of during her stay with them. She jumped in the enormous eclectic shower one last time, with both dogs on the two bath mats next to her, gathered her belongings and prepared to leave to return back to her apartment on the northwest side. Whenever she arrived back at her own place there was a sense of relief and melancholy, as she knew that nothing in her rented abode was hers. She still hadn't purchased any furniture for her own living needs since returning from the island, feeling as though she would up and move again, but the house sitting jobs were putting a damper on those needs. She loaded the rolling olive and headed out the door. She managed to leave the back door open so the two dogs had plenty of room to roam and the freedom to go in and out. What she did notice was her suitcase tag had been chewed to pieces. "When did that happen?" she said while gazing at the doe-eyed little beagle. The dog had an adorable way of tilting her head, as if to know she was up to no good, and wanted to leave her one last piece of mischief before she headed home. She felt a bit sad to walk away from the animals that were in her care for any length of time. Not only did they whine as she walked out the door, locking it behind her, but she could hear them howling while driving down the road. It made her start to want her own dog again.

She woke up next to William and excitedly exclaimed "I'm ready to explore Morocco!" He had an intensely restless evening, his legs kicking all over the place and sighing most of the night, while she pretended not to hear or feel any of it. She was a light sleeper though, and heard everything. Her dreams were extremely vivid and included far out images, from water to cockroaches to big ships, to teaching aerobics, to her teeth falling out, the large packs of wolves protecting her, and that praying mantis dream, which is the one that mostly got her attention. Her spirit was on full alert. He always had to question her motives when she was talking about an adventure. He knew the old Rachel would get up and go. He wasn't so clear on the new Rachel. She shared her dream images with him again, mainly because she wanted to engage him in her crazy mind a bit more and figure out how it applied to her daily life or future goals. He just shook his head, as his practical self was doing his own figuring out about new clients for the direction his career was headed, the receipts he had to log into his ledger, and making sure that his clothes were neat and ready to go for his next appointment. They were such different animals, through and through. It was when she named the ever-growing zit on her neck "Priscilla" that he was reassured just how different they were. "It has a mind of its own" she said happily, while examining it in the mirror and using as much concealer to cover it up so it wouldn't stand out under the fluorescent lights at the vitamin job. "Are you stressed out?" he asked in a serious tone, trying to hide his laughter at her closeness to the mirror and messing with Priscilla. "Not really, just feel like I'm constantly giving to so many people and things these days" she said in a mundane voice. "Priscilla and I have a big day today, writing and standing on concrete floors all day" she told him, still joking and having some fun. He loved her so much that he didn't think twice about her naming a pimple and having its own identity. He just accepted it as part of Rachel.

Taking a vacation together was wildly different than going on an adventure or exploring a new country or place. She talked about so many wild fantasies of the two of them camping together in some remotely wooded area, full of wolves howling at night, nothing but the clearest skies and brightest stars, and snuggling up next to a camp fire with skewered veggies and hot cocoa. He preferred the hotel and resort lifestyle. Ever since his own past of sleeping in the forests and deserts of the war he wanted to enjoy white linen sheets, maid service, and complimentary breakfasts. She understood his past and also took pleasure in the same luxuries, but she wanted to remain true to herself with a weekend of roughing it. Morocco was just one of the latest countries she had expressed a desire to visit. There was always Spain, Australia, South America, New Zealand, and of course any island with the clearest aqua waters. "Where do you plan to get all the money and time?" he asked, in his usual logical way. "If I put it out there to the Universe then I will make it happen" she retorted back quite defensively. She felt she needed to keep her boundaries intact with their conversations. They would agree to disagree, but oftentimes, he felt her ideas were so farfetched that he couldn't understand how her brain was thinking. She felt it didn't require much thinking on her part. If she had a modest plan, enough money to make the plane flight, she would leave the rest up to chance. She had done it before countless times in the past "why should a future trip be any different?" she though while in the shower. He then began to express his insecurity within the relationship. The last time she took off William was left behind for a few months, while she tended to her wanderlust spirit. They did communicate on that adventure for a few weeks, but it wasn't the same as being in person. "He was married at the time though, so it didn't count" she mentioned to Annabelle in a recent conversation. Annabelle was only a phone call away whenever she was spinning out. It went both ways, as Annabelle had her own stuff to deal with, and Rachel would counsel her on the woes of the day. Either way, they understood each other and no words were ever left unsaid. "Would you quit your job?" Annabelle asked in a seriously curious tone. "Well, I would still have the writing and dog-sitting gigs to keep me afloat" she responded in a dreamily manner. "If you think you can take off for a length of time, be without your man, and complete your latest project in solidarity, I say go for it" was the supportive Annabelle answer. "I think I would miss him way too much, have that desire and passion for him, but kind of like it at the same time" she said with her head in the clouds. "You two have grown so close together, how could you leave him?" Annabelle continued in her own logical tone. She was the yin to Rachel's yang. It was clear they were going to go round and round on this topic until Annabelle felt she needed to think it through. Rachel, on the other hand, needed to explore some more. She was feeling a bit unfulfilled in the college city, with the traffic increasing, the skies continuously grey, and the air thick with humidity. She wanted the ocean breeze, the sound of seagulls, the ability to walk to a quaint health food store and buy her tidbits for the day, and write to her heart's content. Annabelle understood this dream, yet still grilled her on how she planned to go about it. "I'm not entirely sure yet, but some dreams never die" she said back to her, with an intent to move forward with her plan.

And, a plan it was. She wasn't taking any flack for her ability to have a free ranging spirit. It was her essence. It was in her DNA. She was going to see it through, leave Annabelle scratching her head analyzing it all, and hopefully take him along for the ride.

Shadows

As with any emerging relationship there is the startling discovery that everyone has a dark side. She was discovering that embracing the unknown-and possibly known-aspects of oneself took plenty of courage and fortitude in order to let it go. Any negative traits also made up the complete wholeness of a person, as she found out over time. Spending more time with William was not only showing her more negative traits within herself, but also highlighting how she interacted in a relationship. She didn't like what she was seeing and feeling all the time. Her lessons in their newfound beginning was teaching her that she wasn't perfect, she didn't have all the answers, and she definitely needed to work on more than she thought. Since she had gone through years of her own personal self-growth and discovery, she was sure that the lessons were over, the struggles were behind her, and the obstacles had been overcome. Living in Bali showed her a side of herself, which she basically thought that was all she needed to know. She would get all sweaty just thinking about any negative traits that she still possessed. When she would ask other people their perceptions of her "C'mon be honest, when you see me what do you see?" was her standard question to her nearest and dearest. She never asked her family, as they were always so distant that the silence pretty much said it all for her. She felt they had their own work to do, and it wasn't her job to fix them, rescue them, or beg for their attention. Those days were over. Her strength lied within her own being, but she needed to know what her friends saw as a weakness about her. Most of her acquaintances would simply say "you are so positive and inspirational, why would you want to change a thing?" Yet, she knew that those weren't her true friends. She wanted to know more about the nuts and bolts of her dark side. Only her closest friends would be honest enough to share what they felt was possibly holding her back from being the most complete and loving woman she needed to be. She didn't need to pose any questions to him, as she always felt a balance of her dark and light side within his presence. It was her shadowed self that needed work. The control, the little lies, and the remnants of passive-aggressive behavior were what she needed to face and with time and work, release into the Universe. She was under the impression that having any dark side was a bad thing, yet it made up who she was, at least that is what she recently read in a new book she purchased from the spirituality section of the book store. It was as if the book just leaped from the shelf and called her name. She wasn't even thinking about buying a book that day; she was simply accompanying him on his quest to find a book he was looking for. But she ended up with a book that made her think. "If I can pay attention to these aspects of myself, give them some weight, then I will be much more able to realize that it is part of who I am, and not give them as much credence" was her subconscious telling her something all the time with each passing chapter. She meditated even more on letting go, and felt okay with it not being perfect. She was more than ready to face the shadows to become an even more whole human being, and she had William to thank for it. She didn't even want to fight it or repress it. "It's almost too exhausting to go there" she texted Rebecca, after they hadn't spoken in weeks, but sorely needed a catchup conversation real time.

They left the bookstore and the reflections of where she was in her life began pouring in again. She wasn't waking up at 2:30 in the morning any more, full of anxiety and confusion. That was his job now. He was at a crossroads with everything he knew about himself, his career, his friends, his passions, his family, and even Rachel. "Self-discovery takes a long time to deal with and understand," she casually mentioned to him on the ride home. "You are in the early stages and it only becomes more painful, more eye-opening, and more fulfilling," she continued. He just drove the truck with nary an expression on his face or words to offer, focusing on the road en route back to his apartment.

William Jameson was an old soul with a challenged beginning. He was a mid-western boy, born into a household with two strict, bible-thumping, conservative parents, who made their money in the oil and gas industry. He was born premature weighing only three pounds, as he gracefully forced his way out into the world. His mother wasn't that excited or keen on having another baby at that time in her life, as four years had lapsed since her first born. She was too busy decorating their many houses all over America, going to the country club, and spending time with their only daughter, who was the apple of her eye. He was named after his father, with many expectations to live up to being the only future man of the house. He was told to protect, guide, and earn enough to support a household. He came from money. His parents traveled the world, entertained on a weekly basis, and kept an assortment of collectibles to show off to guests, including the likes of world-famous athletes and scholars. He always felt like he had some big shoes to fill. Not only did he have a rough start as a youth, an early heart condition that left him with a large scar in the center of his chest, but he found himself in many fights trying to survive the constant barrage of not being good enough for family or friends. He carried this dark cloud with him throughout his entire youth.

When he was finished with high school he made the decision to enlist in the army. He was following in his fathers' footsteps, and his entire family was extremely proud that he chose the military path. Wearing a soldiers' uniform, serving his country, and earning one medal after another for leadership in his platoon was doing his family right. He always did what he was told. Even as a leader in the army at a time when the world was going to one of the costliest wars in America, he kept to the tasks at hand, believed in what Congress and Washington had told him, and did his job to the utmost degree. He had conservative views, serious thinking, and always wanted to please his parents. No amount of goodness and stellar behavior would amount to consciously doing exactly what he was told to do with a guilty conscience. He carried around an immense amount of shame as well. He flitted from one marriage to the next, just trying to do the right and noble thing. Unfortunately, he rushed into relationship situations that had no love, barely any friendship, or even proper courting. He simply married the women because he felt his parents would approve. He never truly loved either of his previous wives; he mainly stayed due to the idea of commitment and the religious upbringing that he was told to follow. He never complained though. He knew that he had a charmed life early on, and attending a prestigious private college after the army was a sure sign that he was going to be a success in business. He graduated with honors late in life, earned his Master's Degree, and continued on the same course as his father. His second wife was also a corporate woman, so both of his parents couldn't be more pleased. Their beginning as a couple was somewhat typical given both of their conservative backgrounds. Neither one wanted kids, so they settled on a dog. His parents weren't thrilled with the idea that no one would carry on the Jameson family name, but he didn't truly love his wife and she never wanted to engage in his wild passionate ways, which was a big problem from the get-go, given his propensity for sensual pleasures.

Many years had passed, his wife called all the shots on where they were to live and what type of church they would attend. He was staking his own claim in business, whereby he was a financial consultant and up-and-coming life coach, albeit struggling to launch a profession with too many past years in the army. He felt that combining the two professions would utilize all his skills and expertise that he harnessed from his military years. Leadership and survival were all that he knew, and with nine years into a loveless marriage, he was an expert at both. His saving grace was his dog. He trained him, loved him, was the sole provider for him, and made sure all his needs were met. His dog gave him the unconditional love that was sorely absent in his upbringing and his marriages. He was a follower in the real world, but a leader in the army and his own mind. During his sixteen years wearing fatigues and giving orders he always felt as though he would never dole out a duty to a fellow soldier unless he could do it himself. No task was too great for him. It was upon his return to conventional living that he became submissive, and deep down it caused him great anxiety. He began to drink more. He suffered from post-traumatic-stress-disorder, a wife who enjoyed yelling, and businesses that weren't too keen on hiring veterans who just returned from the war. Most corporations labeled returning war veterans as mental liabilities and were reluctant to bring them on board. He was in and out of one job after another due to his own inner fire and passions that were showing him that something more fulfilling was out there. He didn't know what that was, but surely some higher up in a corporate setting wasn't cutting it for him anymore, as it felt too similar to his home life and upbringing.

He decided to clean up his act, quit drinking for good, and embarked on a healthy solo existence, despite continuing to share a house with his wife. They slept in separate bedrooms. It was when his world was rocked the day he encountered a quirky, light-hearted woman who sat behind the counter at the local health club, he found himself really questioning his marriage. Her bouncing on the blue Fit ball behind the front desk showed him a carefree spirit, and he wanted to get to know her better. He was ready to stake his own claim in this world and he didn't need his parents or his wife to give their approval.

"I think we need to label our sex life exactly what it is," she said one morning after an early run. He was researching some business stuff on the computer, which always put him in an intensity trance, and she just needed to get some emotions off her chest. Her timing on matters of the heart was always when he was caught off guard; so to give his undivided attention wouldn't amount to much. "Do you think that my waning libido could be a problem down the road?" she started to chatter aimlessly. "I mean, I've heard that some women in their 50's can actually pick up their drive with the help of releasing more anxiety and stress in their lives, and not relying solely on hormone replacement therapy" she continued, while he turned his chair in her direction, but desperately wanted to continue his computer research. "I feel I have opened up so much in the emotional department" her voice was still going a mile per minute. "Well, I've tried to understand the whole menopause thing, and since I'm still getting the whys and how's of it, I thought it would help you to not delve into love-making so much." "You know, give your body a chance to recover and whatnot" he caringly replied. "Hmmm, okay, that is most appreciated, but I also need to know that you are satisfied as well" she thankfully said, almost surprising herself with being aware of his needs. Their intimate encounters of late were quickies, at odd times, not much kissing involved, and the same words uttered over and over again in the moment of climax. He just wanted to feel connected to her, yet she needed a little more romantic foreplay. Both were sort of switching roles a bit. In the early days it was he who wanted to spend a great amount of time making sure that she was satisfied, feeling pleasured and somewhat dirty. With the recent pressures of spending more time together coupled with her menopausal phase in life, it didn't bode well for their sexual intimacy. She wasn't as turned on at all hours of the day like she used to be in their beginning. If anything she retreated a bit, given the fact her body was changing, she was tired more often, and he was going through his own transformation. The same page they were on weeks after their reconnect romantic vacation in Mexico suddenly turned into a bit of a chore. The only bright spot of their togetherness was the experimenting with different recipes on a new diet. She had chosen the vegan lifestyle for so long, but was willing to explore the options of introducing animal protein back into her diet, mainly because he was eating grass-fed meat and it intrigued her. She loved to cook and he was a warm recipient of all her nutrition ideas, habits, and innovations. Cooking was never a chore to her at all. The notion of this new Paleo diet was a lifestyle he was now embracing, and she was all too excited to step into the domestic role with several creative dishes. It made her feel useful, needed, and kind of sexy in a way. If anything, she felt it might spark her libido to get into action.

But they were in another stage of their partnership. "Are we getting boring?" she had curiously posed the question to Annabelle in one of their weekly chats regarding her and William. Annabelle, being somewhat of the female archetypal character of him, responded with her own sensibilities about sex and making love "When he wants to label your intimacy with his own words, you have to allow that" she would say in a calm and insightful manner. "I get that completely; it's just that I need more hugs and kisses than going straight to the act" she replied in a somewhat hopeless and modest manner. She was trying to convey to Annabelle how she has evolved in her own right. Annabelle understood and sensed her emotions, but was being her usual, practical self. It was exactly how he was and it showed Rachel her dark side. She felt she could admit it. She would hopefully understand it, claim it then release it. "At least that's what all the books on the subject professed" she mentioned to Annabelle.

She punched out on the vitamin job and saw his truck in the parking lot with some genuine excitement that he was there waiting for her. She felt like they were in high school going out on their first date. The art gallery was only blocks away and she knew that attending an art opening would be a positive step in networking in the community and showing support for one of her dog-sitting clients. He was showcasing many of his oil on canvas pieces, and both of them had never been to that type of event together. It felt new. It felt authentic. He loved oil paintings and he felt they could both benefit from attending. Driving around the nearby neighborhood and finding the perfect parking spot wasn't his strong suit. If anything, it infuriated her just how patient he was with going around block after block in search of the safest curb to perform some kind of parallel maneuvering. The eclectic neighborhood was full of small colorfully decorated homes, front porches dolled up like pictures out of *Town and Country* magazine, and hipster people walking around at all hours of the night. She hadn't visited that side of town since college. It was odd to her. She worked at the vitamin job which was only a few blocks away. "Why have I never been here?" she mused to him. He didn't hear her. When he finally decided on his parking spot she was so ready to leap out of the truck and be part of the art gallery scene that she forgot it took him an equally long time to just get out of the truck. People were standing outside sipping on their glasses of wine, wearing their cool art opening outfits, and talking to each other as if they truly cared what the other person was saying. Conversations at art gallery openings were always a bit uncomfortable. "How long do you want to stay at this thing?" he asked, as they were walking to the front door. "Just long enough to say hi to Mike and Chris, observe a few paintings, pretend we can afford them, then linger on out the door," she replied in kind of a know-it-all manner. "Okay then, no worries, but should we have some sort of signal if we get separated and we are ready to bail" he asked her, as if allowing her to take the lead. He had been to a few gallery openings in his own right, so he was well versed on the ins and outs of when to leave, who to shake hands with, and how each conversation would go. Plus he was hungry, and the event only had a table with small warm quiches and tidbits that would never satisfy his raging metabolism. She assured him they would only stay long enough to show their presence and support then go grab a bite to eat at the nearby cool and trendy eatery.

She spotted Mike and Chris in the middle of the crowd. Most of the attendees were young, hip, and knew the highlighted artists showing their work. Mike was the artist and Chris was his partner. Together they had hired her to look after their beloved dog for a solid week at their architecturally-designed home. She loved every minute of being in their house, walking the dog several times per day, sleeping with the pooch at night hot flashes and all, writing every morning in the airy bright office, and listening to piped-in "groove salad" music from their fancy stereo. "That is another synchronicity right there" she happily exclaimed to him on the phone one day. "The groove salad theme was strangely similar to our romantic music in the hotel room in Mexico" she continued. "I'm definitely meant to be here in this house watching this adorable dog" she exhaustedly continued giving him cauliflower ear.

As they perused the many pieces of oil paintings in the small, concrete, seemingly hollow gallery that also doubled as a yoga studio, William and his stomach were ready to go. She had acknowledged Mike and Chris, hugged both of them, thanked them for the invite to the event, and meandered through the hipster crowd holding hands with him out the door. The weirdness of the night continued, as they ventured over to the quaint neighborhood vegetarian eatery, where both of them were simply out of sync. The food didn't even taste that great at this legendary place she used to call her first "real" job back in her early college days. "When my gut is on overdrive, I basically can't chew and swallow food that doesn't satisfy me, and I'm not that hungry anyway," she casually mentioned to him, as he was fidgeting with his fork. "Good thing. Your soup is only $4.00" he flippantly responded, which annoyed her to no end. "Typical that you would balk about the price" she said just to get in the last jab. He didn't say a word.

Whatever was going on in the cosmos was certainly causing a stir and fire in their relationship. He was more obstinate; she was going overboard in expressing herself emotionally. They seemed at a crossroads for all the wrong reasons. The pasts of both of them were coming up and wreaking havoc in their togetherness. Not a moment went by where they were doing the loving, subtleties that all relationships seem to possess. "What the hell is going on with you lately?" she asked him over the phone the following morning after the art opening. "I don't know." "I feel like I can sense stuff, and right now I'm thinking that we aren't on the same page, like you have your own agenda" he sullenly responded. They had a rather weird evening post gallery outing, which ended with them having a conversation in his truck, kissing, hugging, and making a plan for the following day. He dropped her off at her apartment and left to go home. He didn't even want her to spend the night. In her gut she had a sense that something wasn't right. They even spoke at length on the phone after they went their separate ways, and still her intuition was on high alert. She never saw what was coming next. He was so intense and seemed so full of angst that night, and she was deflecting and dodging all his blames and suspicions. It was as if they had taken one giant step backwards in their partnership. "Is he trying to push me away on purpose?" she went outside and looked up to the sky for answers. She loved gazing at the clouds on her walks. She would make out shapes and signs within each woven layer of cottony billows high in the blue sky. It eased her mind and gave her a sense that she was safe and someone was always watching over her. "I need some answers here!" she demanded to the Universe. Patience wasn't always her strong suit, and this time it felt as though she wanted to further her growth in this partnership with him, but didn't quite know what the next step should be.

She ventured over to his apartment, knocked on the door, and nothing more was said. After their mad passionate love the following morning, she couldn't help but watch him. His three-day old scruff gave her the chills. It was so out of character that he allowed himself to be unkempt. She loved it. She loved his smell. He had the best smell, around his nose, on his forehead, his throat, and throughout his burly chest. Even his sweaty smell aroused her, and when she mentioned it to close friends, they thought she was crazy. She could bury herself in his body and feel completely okay for the rest of her life. As he was busying himself with the morning chores she simply watched. She had been up a few hours prior to him, so she was already a step ahead of him in the routine department. It was every ounce of him that led her to practically maul him at his desk chair. He was so enthralled by the forthright and control that he just let her take over and direct their lovemaking. The light bulb went off in her head. "We are exactly where we need to be," she whispered in a serious and sensual tone in his ear, while clumsily licking his ear. He wasn't entirely convinced, as his own insecurities were rearing their ugly heads regarding the relationship. "Oh, you think so?" his lower-consciousness side responded. "Personal growth has a way of dredging up the deep-rooted vulnerabilities of any individual" she wisely mentioned to him, and he was smack dab in the middle of his own learning curve. Ironically, she was in the same boat.

She snuck up behind him as he was intensely gazing at the computer screen, gave him a solid kiss on the cheek, laced up her shoes and off she went for a run. He stayed behind to tend to his affirmations and meditation of the day. He was still reeling from how forward she was in her actions that particular morning, and he wondered if he was over-thinking it. "Aye, just let it go and appreciate who she is and what her intentions were" was his own subconscious getting the best of him.

She returned from her sweaty, humid run and found him in a total state of confusion and surrender. He hadn't worked in months, was on a six-month sabbatical of his own doing, and was actually contemplating giving up. "You cannot give up!" she said firmly with a sense of wisdom. "I swore my entire last five years of my life that whatever happened and whichever way my life was going, I would not give up," she continued in an older woman kind of way. She certainly had a "been-there-done-that" kind of attitude about her the past many days. The exchanges of words and emotions between them were so charged for weeks that she knew they were on the brink of another level and higher form of intimacy, and giving up was not in the cards. She called it the "epitome of relating bliss". "I just feel that my leaving the corporate world and venturing out on my own right now might not be such a good idea in this economy" he said with that same sullen look on his scruffy face from earlier. "I've got to hit it hard today and make sure that either I stay on task with my goals, or go work for someone else like I've done in the past" he continued, as if to include her in on his affirmations of the day. "You just have to trust your gut, and so far my gut is telling me that you can be that person who helps others with their financial fitness" as she put it so eloquently. When he left the corporate world he wanted to go down a path that would allow him more freedom, more ability to travel with her, a nice house with a swimming pool, and somewhere close to the ocean. Both of them had the same dream. Both of them knew that living near the sea would be their destiny. And both of them knew that it would take great obstacles to overcome with vast amounts of hope and faith. She was on the brink of getting another book published, and her yearly efforts of writing for wellness publications, blogs, and small health books would pave the way for her own success. She was tireless in her efforts to help others through the written word. As somewhat of a shy person in the speaking world, she could spread her ideas of life, healing, and health through her books. That was her intent, her mission, and her reasons for being in the world. He, on the other hand, was a natural born leader and a man of service. After his own rough beginning and setbacks, he knew that his purpose was also to help others, and it would happen with guiding people on their own financial means to living well into retirement and remaining true to themselves. He knew the ins and outs of money. He knew how to make it, invest it, save it, and show others the best way to their own personal freedom. His only hiccup now was his motivation in encouraging others down a path he wasn't so sure he was confident in doing himself. Their lives together were so parallel and mirroring at a stage of their togetherness that she wanted to pursue the intimacy even further. To him it meant seeing each other more. To her it meant maximizing the time they spent together in constructive powerful conversations that tapped into their very core. Every time she teetered on the edge of her lengthy words with him he would submit for a few minutes, only to realize that the depths of their exchanges made him uncomfortable. It was then that she realized they can only grow from that place. Facing their shadows within the partnership would benefit each individual and show them their true selves. Deconstructing the very process of who they were in order to build them back up was driving her to major distraction. She not only suggested they take a road trip to the west coast together to visit and meet her family, but possibly incorporate a spiritual workshop at the final destination. He was on board and made a few phone calls, then slunk in his chair for a bit. "I am spending so much money on therapy, mentors, and spiritual healers at this point that I don't know how much more I can take before I learn to trust my own instincts and process" he emphatically told her as she was preparing to go home. "Just think about it," she said to him. "I feel that this will be such a win-win for both of us" she continued in her usual chatty kind of way.

It took her an extra half hour to get in her car and drive home, as she didn't want to leave him high and dry with no closure from their earlier conversation. She was still dripping sweat from her run, but he was priority, as were his emotions and feelings. He blew her a kiss from his balcony and she sped away knowing that her manuscript awaited her, as well as standing all day on her feet on the hard floors at the clock-punching job. He went back to his computer to continue with more research. He didn't want to leave any stone unturned.

Driftwood

The transformation happening between them was on full court press. He was going through a metamorphosis and so was she. How they were relating with their intimacy, their fears, their highs and lows; it was all up for grabs. In her wildest dreams she would never imagine that where they began, and how they began, would turn out to be as intense and awesome. Her own personal growth over the years, through her countless relationships and two failed marriages, she was finally in a love partnership with a man who had his own failed marriages, his own charred beginnings, and on a miraculous path that had put them together in the same space and time. It was no coincidence. "Everything happens for a reason" she told her mother. She felt the Universe had set it up from the onset of their births. It took complications, severed ties, drama, karmic cleanses, and differing personalities to realize that they were meant to be traveling down the path together. "I don't view any of my past as a failure, and I sure as hell have no regrets" she told him while brushing her teeth, her mouth full of toothpaste. She vowed never to travel alone throughout the remainder of her journey. She had done that for so many years. If she ever felt the need to explore or take an adventure she wanted him along for the ride. He felt the same way. They didn't possess each other. They no longer had the power struggles that dominated the onset of their new beginning. They were working in harmony and peace. They took responsibility for all their actions. They owned their stuff. They talked about everything that would constitute and seal their togetherness. They compromised after actually processing what the other one needed. Loving William was transforming Rachel, and vice versa. They were one. There were no exits.

One morning while she was rousing herself into her routine and self-care for the day, a rock on her shelf caught her eye and she recalled her time in Nicaragua. She thought fondly of Jonathan and their many interactions and friendship in that foreign country. She distinctly remembered sitting on the sand at low tide and leaning up against a large old piece of driftwood. "It must have been there for many years, or it simply washed up to shore in the middle of the night" she thought while applying frankincense oil to her third eye. She hadn't seen so much large cumbersome driftwood ever in her life. Even when she was the high-dollar real estate agent showing luxury property to clients in Southern California many moons ago, pieces of driftwood never caught her eye on the beach, if they were even there. It was as if Jonathan had to point out and capture in photograph all the stranded pieces of driftwood on the long stretches of sand. The scenery changed every morning on that beach in Nicaragua. "Where did all the big pieces of driftwood come from?" she asked him during a sunset conversation while watching the last-remaining surfers coming in from the sea. He never truly responded in a way that she would understand. Maybe she didn't pay attention long enough to get the meaning that he was conveying. She wasn't even sure she heard him and had to go and figure it out for herself. What she does remember was being mesmerized by how large each piece was and the beauty and stories that such big pieces of driftwood might convey. They showed up in different spots every single day on that beach in Central America. Some were so big that they were sort of hindrances on the sand. Even when she left Nicaragua after 10 days of life-changing occurrences, she never gave it a second thought. With William now in her life in the deepest loving way she reflected on that entire experience in the foreign country. The driftwood was her sign that life flows and comes and goes in every instance. Jonathan was a catalyst for her to understand herself on a different level, and he was merely put in her life to highlight her talents as a creative writer, expanding and growing in literary ways, nothing more. The driftwood had stories to tell. She was in the midst of her own greatest love story ever. "Call it Divine intervention, if you will" she mentioned to a coworker at the vitamin job. She had given her notice that day, punched out for the last time, and drove the rolling olive westward home, with lingering driftwood memories in her psyche.

It had been the most dramatic forty-eight hours that she had ever experienced in any relationship. The scene was playing out all over again. "It has actually been over six years since I've had any kind of roller-coaster relationship, period!" she texted to Annabelle. Once again Annabelle was her savior in the recent ongoing relationship growth and frustration between Rachel and William. After all she was in a good space with her young massage lover, and again was more than willing to offer any words of wisdom that she could at that time. She woke up with such a headache the following morning. He had shown her his dark side. Both of them reeling from the experience and he continued to pull away and take care of his own heart. It was the least he could do, as she was confusing him with her words and actions. "I don't know if I'm scared of someone controlling me, or just needing my independence, or both" she continued the texting with Annabelle, trying to keep up. The two women finally chatted on the phone about the ordeal. She was on another dog-sitting job and trying to juggle the idiosyncrasies of both dogs, while he needed her attention at that moment. The cranberry kombucha drink she bought on her last day at the vitamin job exploded on the kitchen counter and everything in sight was saturated with a crimson, bubbly mess. "Probably shouldn't have left it in the warm car" she carelessly thought to herself while using every towel in sight to soak up the liquid. Her computer was right in the line of fire and the fizzy liquid jeopardized her laptop battery. There was glass everywhere, the dogs were hiding due to the sound of the unexpectedly loud blast, and he wouldn't let up. It put her over the edge. She tried to maintain her own center, but he was bound and determined to throw her off. She ended up hanging up on him. He hung up on her a few times. It was chaos at its best. They were in a full-blown power struggle again. "Argh, I can't do this right now!" she raised her voice To Annabelle while the poor dogs were still snuggling up behind the television, so as not to think they were in trouble.

"Just breathe with me," said Annabelle in a wonderful soft tone. She was cleaning up the mess, yet her heart was pumped full of adrenaline. She wanted so badly for him to understand her, to truly know that she had some writing deadlines, that her dog-sitting side jobs brought her so much joy, that she wished they would live together in a cozy neighborhood with their own dog and walking distance to everything quaint and wonderful. "Is this a pipe dream?" she willfully asked one of the dogs in her care. The dog was just warming up to her after a slow and fearful start. It took a few hours before the dog was walking freely and happily next to her and even sleeping with her in bed. She still had a way with dogs, despite her energy feeling compromised. "All I can think about is that driftwood and the meaning," she softly said to the dog still coiled behind the T.V. desperately trying to woo him out and feel more comfortable.

"I want to see you and talk to you in person" she said to him in an email before she went to bed on that rainy night with the temporary dog by her side. She put on an eye cover pillow she found in the nightstand and had one dream after another. It had been an uncharacteristically intense past few days with him, and she woke up with one headache after another. She was pumping her body full of natural headache pills she got at discount from the vitamin store and constantly readjusting her perfect pillow to accommodate her chronically sore neck; but the source of her tension was her emotions. Even she knew it deep down inside. No amount of pills or adjustment pillows would alleviate the nagging feeling that she herself was going through growing pains and transformation with him. She was feeling "cagey", as one of her coworkers had so eloquently put it; not wanting to give up the independent parts of her that she had worked so desperately on over the years. He was pulling out all the stops. But she had an idea; one that she felt was so compelling and in-the-moment that she couldn't wait to share it with him. "It would solve so much of our recent woes and intensity," she wrote to Annabelle in an email. There was no answer from the other end of the email, and it was just as well. Emails and Annabelle took a bit longer to answer than the usual text rant. She wanted to position herself on her yoga mat and clear the noise in her head. It was either that or she would go for a solid run in her neighborhood, whereby she could process her thoughts. The weather was unreal outside, crispness in the air, birds singing so loudly, and a feeling of expansiveness. As she sat on the toilet leaning over and rubbing her feet she knew what she needed at that moment. She harnessed her wild curly hair into a ponytail, laced up her shoes, and ventured out the door.

Singing a lyric or two from Fleetwood Mac songs gave her all kinds of creative energy on her run. "You could be my silver spring" was one melody that carried her up a steep hill. "We can make it happen" was another lyric from an old 80s Chicago tune, which took her glistening body all the way home to stretch. "I found a quarter and a penny!" she excitedly texted him after she unlocked her door to her sublet. Annabelle had also emailed her back in her wonderfully insightful way that gave Rachel a reason to smile. So many thoughts were rumbling around her brain and she wanted to get them down on paper before she forgot them. He had given her a small tape recorder early on to help her if she ever forgot to jot down any inspirational thoughts that came to her while she was out and about. He was so supportive of her writing career that he even dubbed himself a "groupie." What struck her as perplexing was "how could he be an advocate of me being a full-time writer when he is jeopardizing my time, which is the very thing a writer needs?" Too many unanswered thoughts were spinning in her head, creating more noise than she truly wanted. "I'm just going to let it all go and surrender" she said to herself while looking in the mirror, this time applying lavender oil to every chakra. She sat down to compose an email to her mother, which was long overdue. Her Mom had been visiting her niece and was about to become a great grandmother. As beautiful and heartwarming as that sounded to Rachel she couldn't wrap her head around being there with them at that time. Maybe her not having any children hardened her to those lifetime events. Maybe she just didn't feel that connected to her former sister-in-law, who was now living with another man besides Rachel's long lost brother. Maybe she felt embarrassed that she never had children of her own and her mother would inevitably remind her, or maybe she was so embroiled in her own interpersonal relationship growths that she just didn't have time to include the joys of others. "Am I being selfish?" she asked William one evening. His answer was not something she wanted to hear. All sorts of questions came up for her, as she felt so far removed from her family. They were too emotionally distant from the get go, and all her past foibles and challenges perpetuated even more distance. They just never got her.

She spent the next few mornings writing up a storm. She submitted a few articles to her favorite blog site, ended up putting out some more emotional fires with William, and thought about the great idea she wanted to propose to him before they got further embroiled in their togetherness.

"Let's go on a road trip!" she said to him on the phone that evening. He was already in frustration mode that they were spending another day apart, but given her writing deadlines and zest for publishing another story, she had work to do. Writing was a solitary and somewhat introverted life for her. She never imagined it would be that way, but she also never imagined her falling in love with a man who broke her walls down and always gave her something new to think about. Giving up the vitamin job was an avenue for her to spend more time with him, conjure up more stories for her blog and book, and plan one excursion after the next. The dog sitting money was always appreciated and welcomed, but her real freedom came through her written word. Taking a road trip with him would open up new doors for both of them. He had some upcoming seminars in his newly adopted field of study, so it would be the only opportunity they would have to see a part of the country where she used to call "home". "I think road tripping to California would be so cool, you can meet my family, friends, and we can take our time. It could be something new that we shared and who knows where that will lead?" she hurriedly said on the phone to him, so as not to lose her thought. "I have a workshop at the end of July, but I need to be able to take an important Skype call in mid-June." "I'm not sure I can be on the road during that time where I might not get quality cell phone coverage" he said after listening to her brilliant idea. "Why don't we take two weeks, and leave after your call, and after my dog sitting job that's coming up mid-month of June?" she responded in a compromising way. He agreed that a road trip would be so good for them. He was still jockeying for ways to spend more time together, and the fact that she came up with this partnered idea sounded pretty wonderful to him. He felt like she was starting to see the bigger picture of him and her. He felt like she was making an effort. And most of all he felt like she wanted to be with him. She always took solo road trips in the past. With her previous nomadic ways she was always venturing out year after year to some distant city and never looking back. With thoughts of driftwood meandering back in her mind, she was determined not to leave him behind, and accomplish more than what meets the eye, meeting her family and friends.

The Velvet Cat

"I had an incredible water dream whereby I was swimming in some beautiful aqua-watered cove, in the deep end and this very large whale came out of this dark hole. I think it was a whale. It was big, though. It looked powerful, and it made me feel all sorts of emotions. As if the wave of water was carrying me away with the whale. Then, I was in this small car camper, which was perched on top of a hill. As we all started to fall asleep the entire camper began to shake and rumble and I realized we were detached from the car and rolling down the hill towards the water. The camper floated for a bit then kind of sank, but not really. I checked the contents of my little suitcase and everything was dry and intact. Then, I woke up." She jotted down this entire memorable dream.

"My feelings of fatigue and exhaustion stem from being stretched in about a hundred different directions. Granted, only one of my responsibilities was the clock-punching job, but I adore caring for others' dogs in their homes. I love writing when the creative mood strikes and I feel like when I'm with William, I'm torn between my own dark side, and the light that wants to emerge. The man pushes my buttons in a good way. I need to look at my own repressed emotions. I need to experience the growth and honesty of value within me. I need to know that we can hug for hours after an intense conversation. I have come this far to understand what I need. He and I are on parallel paths. I've said it a hundred times, but it's truly sinking in. Maybe that's what the dream was about. Being stable and secure in a camper, yet rolling down the hill to water to allow what I'm feeling to truly sink in. This is what comes to mind. I have nothing but gratitude and continued hope that this is the best path right now. All the signs and synchronicities are ever-present." She continued on with paragraph after vivid paragraph, writing furiously in her journal that morning.

"I saw a yellow butterfly randomly fly by. Every song that I stumble onto, every coin on the road, every color that graces my presence, the words and phrases that people post on Facebook, the animals in one situation after another, messages in a book, nuances about William and what he does and says, things my friends are going through, and just the general sense that life is okay-this is carrying me through each day. My dreams have been going off! The praying mantis dream, causing me to pay attention to everything in the moment gave me pause. The platypus dream, showing me change is happening within my life; the little frogs on the stairs jumping at me and conjuring up the very same emotion. I feel like it's all coming together, like a well-played out symphony. As I've walked through this maze of life, finding my way, and surviving all the struggles and my own curious choices I am on the cusp of something really great; something that philosophers describe as "ultimate destiny." I am positioned in this life of mine, and it only gets better. How I can help people to be authentic and true to themselves is front and center, if only everyone would realize that it's okay to be who they are. My internal message is coming forth. My insides are screaming that this is a year of transformation within us all and Mother Earth. I am about as happy and content as a girl can be. Yes, I'm a girl in my 50s; still plugging along with a childlike heart; still enjoying movement that brings me joy, despite my body not always agreeing with my brain. But I will never give up. I will always feel that my heart is out there and willing to give to anyone who lets the message in. Thank you, God, for giving me this experience. I'm humbled knowing you are constantly at my side. See it. Know it. Trust it. Good morning!!!"

The long journal entry on a crisp blue perfect spring morning depicted her excitement. So much so that she just had to share it with the pages in front of her at that moment and not miss a beat. She kept forgetting the little tape recorder, so she hurried home to sit down and write what her latest thoughts were. And they were moving fast. She wrote all the time. All that sneaking around of paragraphs on the computer at the vitamin job when she was supposed to be helping customers with their sleep problems, now paved the way for more freedom with her words and time.

The latest pressures within her relationship with William gave her the impetus to finally declare "I need some alone time". She felt a writer needs space to produce quality work. "A girl writer will always leave, but she will always come back too, stronger than before" she read somewhere in a blog. She needed to tell him that her awesome idea of a road trip had to be matched with some solitude prior to the trip. "This isn't going to be a walk in the park," she mentioned to Annabelle, who had a handle on the Taurus personality. "We will be spending two solid weeks together just like we did in Mexico, but I have to get what's in my heart out there" she continued to proclaim to a compassionate Annabelle. "You go girl!" Annabelle admittedly responded to a surprised Rachel. The two of them were sort of the yin and yang of each other, and Annabelle was more like a female William to Rachel. "Well, I'm at my wits ends with a story and honestly my crotch could use a break" she continued, as if to justify why she needed some alone time. Because he was such a passionate lover she always mentioned to him that she needed some recovery time between their lovemaking sessions. "I'm no spring chicken anymore" she would say, with respect to her abilities to keep a libido. Her words were palpable and sincere, and before she hung up the phone with Annabelle she mentioned the possibility that a visit to her neck of the woods might be forthcoming. That entire coastline in Northern California, with the sweeping drops into the ocean, whales breaching far out in the Pacific, one garden after another lining the highways, colors so bright that Van Gogh would turn over in his grave, which is where she wanted to take him. She had so many friends who lived there and some incredible memories with that place in general. Southern California always had its appeal to Rachel, yet it beckoned her in different ways.

Bouncing between thoughts of where to go in California were occupying her mind. One minute she proposed that they visit Northern California, the next minute she was thinking southern California might be more suitable for both of them to squander their road trip days closer to the ocean and warmth. The northern area was mountainous and colder, but the awestruck beauty far surpassed the southern parts of the state. He wanted the beach and sun and vibe. He envisioned them dangling their feet in the ocean, even though water temperatures hovered in the sixties on a summer day. It was more of a wetsuit environment than the tropics. Her brother had a house there and would be traveling in Europe for a few weeks and the place would be vacant for the two of them to partake in a new adventure. As the newfound information was thrown into the mix she absolutely could not decide which course of action to take for their road trip. "I'll just go for a run and listen to my gut" was her fallback position for any confusion thrown in her face. It wasn't so much a negative, as it was a test for her to actually make a decision, which wasn't her strong suit. Being a diplomatic soul she wanted to appease him, her friends, her family, and most of all herself. But her nature of indecisiveness was always at the forefront. If she were to depend on him to make a decision, it would be like asking a turtle to win a race. His slow-moving and stubborn Taurus ways were definitely the opposite of spontaneous. Sometimes it would take him years to make a clear-cut decision on anything, and that was after hours and hours of research. Not only did it drive her to madness in their early days, but she still had a tendency to rib him about it. Although she had accepted that William was William, as steady as a rock, she also knew that her taking the lead on a road trip decision was the best course of action. Her contacts and networks there were like gold to her, and she wanted to include him in that part of her world: her old stomping grounds.

As she thought long and hard about her place in the world, she couldn't forget her place within the relationship with him. She felt so powerless at times, especially when old behavior patterns set in. She felt as though she couldn't gain any forward momentum with how they were relating. She felt like someday it would all be some sort of dream. "Am I overthinking it again?" she furiously wrote in her journal. "I'm a fifty-three year old woman often reduced to occupying a twenty-year old body and mindset. I bounce from reality to fantasy like a ping pong ball" she continued to write and talk to God. Her journaling was a way for her to stay close to her Higher Power; at least she felt God and her angels were always there and listening. Her passions for living and breathing and forging new ground were taking over. She still wasn't clear whether she was to do it alone or in the presence of another. She would only back burner her life if it meant charting new territory in her emotional intimacy with a relationship. He recently claimed over his long birthday weekend "I've never felt closer to you" despite their continued surge of uncomfortable growth together. She still wasn't sure what the hell was going on. One day they were on the top of the world; the very moment within hours of the day, they could easily have dived to several depths of the sea. She always wanted to retreat to her own corner of the world when things got uncomfortable. "Do you feel the growth we are experiencing will ever subside?" she actually asked him when they were both lying in a semi-unconscious state after making love. He expressed himself through tactile, sensual methods and passion. She just liked to talk. "Is this all part of the plan?" she continued to grind the conversation and her own discomfort into the earth. He was motionless on the floor. He had a few rug burns but nothing a little aloe gel couldn't fix.

It had been raining for days on end, and during this reprieve from work and tedious duties both of them felt as though they needed a break from each other. They were heading to California in less than a month, but their togetherness was tense and downright silly sometimes. She ventured out onto the deck at his apartment and noticed the sky had opened up a bit after the rain. The purple and red hues as the sunset cast its shadow on the clouds overhanging in her direction gave her the impetus to open her arms wide and lean her head back. The ladybug then landed right on her over worn white t-shirt, square in her solar plexus. She looked up and saw that the clouds were forming a perfect heart shape with purplish and red colors outlining the formation. A burst of lightening then graced through the center of the heart-shaped clouds. It was the perfect moment. Her own being sensed the message from the heavens. It silenced her mind and thoughts. She looked down and noticed an unusual looking feral cat lurking around the balcony. It grabbed her attention, so much so that she sidestepped the semi-comatose William on the floor of the apartment and went downstairs to pet it. The cat was as smooth as velvet; a coat so lush that she couldn't imagine it living in the wild with no one to love or care for it. The cat had an empathetic way about it and lingered around her legs and feet. It turned over on its back to expose a sweet white belly that was just as velvety as the top coat. Its humming purrs gave her a great amount of peace and tranquility. He went out onto the balcony to see what was going on, saw her with the cat then waited until she returned inside to unload everything in his heart. His words were real and their feelings were on fire. They embraced hard with tears in their eyes, such compassion and love in their souls, then hugged each other even tighter. Together they loaded up their yoga mats in his truck to join a Sunday morning class just a few miles away, and without saying a word only their hearts were completely full of each other.